PENGUIN MODERN CLASSICS

LE GRAND MEAULNES

Alain-Fournier, christened Henri Alban, was born in La Chapelle d'Angillon (Cher) in 1886, the son of a country schoolmaster. He was educated at Brest and in Paris, where he met and fell in love with the original Yvonne, who influenced his whole life and work. In 1905 he was working in Chiswick, London.

Le Grand Meaulnes (*The Lost Domain*) was published in 1912. *Les Miracles* appeared posthumously in 1924. His important correspondence with Jacques Rivière and his letters to his family were published in 1926 and 1930 respectively.

Alain-Fournier was killed in action on the Meuse in 1914.

ALAIN-FOURNIER

LE GRAND MEAULNES

TRANSLATED BY FRANK DAVISON

PENGUIN BOOKS

Penguin Books Ltd, Harmondsworth, Middlesex, England
Penguin Books Australia Ltd, Ringwood, Victoria, Australia

—

First published in France 1913
This translation first published by
Oxford University Press 1959
Published in Penguin Books 1966
Reprinted 1968, 1970, 1971, 1972

—

Translation copyright © Oxford University Press, 1959

—

Made and printed in Great Britain
by Richard Clay (The Chaucer Press) Ltd,
Bungay, Suffolk
Set in Monotype Garamond

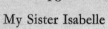

TO
My Sister Isabelle

CONTENTS

PART THREE

PART ONE

THE BOARDER

HE appeared at our house on a Sunday in November 189...

I still say 'our' house though it is ours no longer; nearly fifteen years have passed since we left the neighbourhood, and we shall not be going back to it.

We lived on the premises of the secondary school at Sainte-Agathe. My father, whom I called Monsieur Seurel just like the other boys, was in charge of the upper form where you qualified for a teacher's certificate. He taught the lower form as well, leaving the younger boys to my mother.

It was a long red building standing on the edge of the village. It was draped in virginia-creeper and had five door-windows opening on a very large courtyard used as a playground and partly roofed over as a shelter in bad weather. There was a wash-house on one side, and a huge gateway gave direct access to the village. A smaller gate on the north side of the courtyard opened on the road to the railway station three kilometres distant. To the south, gardens, fields, and meadows stretched away to the boundaries of the commune. This was the setting in which the most troubled and most precious days of my life were lived: an abode from which our adventurings flowed out, to flow back again like waves breaking on a lonely headland.

Some pencil checking the rota, or the decision of some inspector or Prefect, had landed us there, and towards the end of the summer holidays, one day long ago, a farmer's cart, preceding our household goods, set us down, my mother and me, before the rusty little gate. Some children who had been stealing peaches in the garden scuttled off through a gap in the hedge . . . My mother – we called her Millie – the most meticulous housewife ever known, hurried indoors through rooms littered with dust and straw and came to the despairing conclusion, as she did whenever we moved, that our furniture couldn't possibly be fitted into such awkward spaces . . . So out she came to share her woes with me, and while she lamented she kept rubbing away at my childish features with a handkerchief to remove the grime of the journey. Then back again to make an inventory of doors and windows that would have to be blocked before the place was habitable . . . As for me, I stood there on the gravel of this alien courtyard under a wide-brimmed straw hat adorned with ribbons, just waiting, or at most making a tentative survey of the well and the play-ground.

At least that is how I now 'imagine' our arrival, for no sooner do I try to recapture my state of vague expectation on that first evening in our courtyard at Sainte-Agathe than memory conjures up other states of expectation: I see myself, both hands pressed against the bars of the main gateway, anxiously on the look-out for someone who will be striding down the village street. And if I try to visualize the first night I had to spend in my attic room between the store-rooms, my mind evokes other nights: I am no longer alone in the room; a tall shadow moves across the wall, to and fro, restless and friendly. The whole peaceful setting – the school, old Martin's field with its three walnut trees, the garden which after four o'clock was invaded by women visitors – is in my thoughts for ever disturbed, transformed once and for all by the presence of one who completely unsettled our adolescence and who, even when gone from us, gave us no respite.

And yet we had been there ten whole years when Meaulnes first came on the scene.

I was fifteen. It was a cold Sunday in November, the first day which had in it a presage of winter. All day Millie kept fretting at the tardiness of the delivery wagon from the station which was to bring her a hat for the turn of the season. She had sent me to Mass alone, and right up to the sermon, from my seat among the choir boys, I had been craning my neck in the hope of seeing her come in with her new hat on.

In the afternoon too I had to go to Vespers by myself.

'Besides,' she said to appease me, brushing my Sunday suit with her hand, 'even if they'd brought it I dare say I'd have had to spend the whole of my Sunday making it over.'

Our winter Sundays often took the same pattern: in the first light my father would set out for some far-away misty pond to fish for pike from a boat, while my mother, shut away till nightfall in her dusky room, made over her humble toilettes. If she kept out of sight it was for fear some lady of her acquaintance, as poor as herself for that matter and as proud, should catch her at it. And I, home from the afternoon service, could only wait in the chilly dining-room with a book till she opened the door to reveal the results of her labours.

On that particular Sunday there was a commotion in front of the church which delayed my return. A christening had drawn a group of children under the porch. In the Square several of the village men in firemen's uniform had stacked their rifles and stood shivering with cold, stamping their feet while Boujardon, the corporal, got more and more entangled in the intricacies of drill . . .

Then, abruptly, the pealing of the baptismal bells left off – as though someone issuing a joyous summons to a fête had become aware of a mistake in the date, or the parish. Boujardon and his troop, arms now shouldered, went off at a trot with the fire-engine, and I watched them turn into a side street followed by four little boys, their thick soles crunching the twigs on the frozen ground. I didn't dare follow them.

And now no sign of life remained in the village except for the Café Daniel. There, over their glasses, men were engaged in heated discussion; one could hear the muffled rise and fall of voices. So, hugging the low wall of the courtyard which isolated our house from the village, I made my way back to the gate, feeling guilty at being so late.

The gate stood open, and I knew at once that something unusual was happening.

And in fact outside the dining-room door – the nearest of the five door-windows which gave on the yard – a grey-haired woman was bent forward trying to see through the curtains. She was tiny and wore an old-fashioned black velvet bonnet.

13

Her face was thin and refined but consumed with anxiety. At sight of her some strange apprehension made me halt on the first step in front of the gate.

'Where in the world can he have got to?' she was saying, half aloud. 'He was with me not two minutes ago. He'll have inspected the place already – he may have taken himself off...'

At each pause in her monologue she would give three little taps on the window-pane – blows that scarcely made a sound.

For no one had come to let this unknown visitor in. Millie's hat, I thought, has arrived at last and, lost to the world in the depths of the red room, beside a bed strewn with old ribbons and feathers out of curl, she's sewing away, ripping, rebuilding her dubious headgear ... Indeed no sooner had I gone into the dining-room, followed by our visitor, than my mother appeared, both hands supporting on her head a structure of wire, silk, and plumes, all still a trifle unbalanced ... She gave me a smile, her blue eyes looking tired from so much close work in the twilight, and called out, 'Look! I've been waiting to show you ...'

Then, catching sight of a stranger in the big arm-chair on the other side of the room, she broke off in confusion, snatching off the new hat which, during the whole of the ensuing interview, she hugged to her bosom like an inverted nest.

The woman in the black velvet bonnet, holding an umbrella and a leather handbag between her knees, had begun to explain her presence, nodding the while and making with her tongue the noises appropriate to a lady paying a call. She had recovered her poise and, once she began speaking of her son, assumed an air both superior and mysterious which aroused our wonderment.

They had driven over from La Ferté-d'Angillon, fourteen kilometres distant from Sainte-Agathe. A widow, and extremely well-off – so she led us to understand – she had lost the younger of her two sons, Antoine, who had died one night after bathing in a polluted pond with his brother on the way home from school. She had decided to place the elder boy, Augustin, *en pension* with us, as a student in the upper form.

And now she was singing the praises of this new boarder

she offered us, no longer the insignificant little person I had seen at the door peering through the window with the distraught and imploring look of a hen whose wild changeling is missing from the brood.

What she told us, with great complacency, about this son of hers was more than surprising. To please her he would trudge beside the river, bare-legged, for miles and miles just to fetch her the eggs of moorhens and wild ducks which he found in the rushes . . . He also set out bow-nets . . . The other night he had found a snared pheasant in the woods . . .

I who scarcely dared go home with a rent in my smock gave Millie a look . . .

But she was no longer listening to our visitor; she even made a sign for silence, and laying her 'nest' on the table with great care, got up noiselessly as if to take someone by surprise . . .

For overhead, in an odd room where we had dumped some half-scorched fireworks left over from the last Fourteenth of July, an unknown footstep, very sure of itself, was coming and going, shaking the ceiling. Then the steps retreated through the vast and murky lofts towards the disused assistant-masters' rooms where we spread linden leaves out to dry and apples to ripen.

'I heard it before,' Millie said in a whisper, 'in the downstairs rooms. I thought it was you, François, home from church . . .'

No one replied. We were now all three on our feet, with beating hearts. The attic door at the top of the kitchen stairs had opened. Someone came down, walked through the kitchen, appeared in the doorway of the dining-room, and stood there in the dusk.

'Is that you, Augustin?'

It was a tall youth, about seventeen. It was too dark to make out much more than his peasant's hat of felt pushed back on his head and a black smock tightly belted in like a schoolboy's. But I could see that he was smiling . . .

He caught my eye and before anyone could ask for an explanation he said, 'Coming out to the yard?'

For a moment I wavered. Then, as Millie said nothing, I picked up my cap and went over to him. We went out through the kitchen and walked across the yard towards the sheltered part already deep in shadow. In the fading light I glanced up at his angular face with its straight nose and faintly shadowed upper lip.

'See what I found in your attic,' he said. 'Didn't it ever occur to you to have a look in there?'

He held out a little wheel of blackened wood wound about with frayed fuses – the 'sun' or perhaps the 'moon' of last July's display.

'There were two that hadn't gone off. We'll set them off just the same,' he added placidly, as if this would do till something better turned up.

When he threw down his hat I saw that he was close-cropped like a peasant. He was showing me the two fuses with paper wicks which the flame had bitten into, seared, and then abandoned. He stuck the nave of the wheels in the gravel, produced a box of matches – this to my astonishment, for we were not allowed matches – and stooping carefully held a flame to the wicks. Then, taking my hand, he pulled me quickly back.

Coming out of doors with Madame Meaulnes – terms of pension having been discussed and agreed upon – my mother saw two great bouquets of red and white stars soar up from the ground with a hiss. And for the space of a second she could see me standing in a magical glow, holding the tall new-comer by the hand, and not flinching . . .

Once again she had nothing to say.

And that evening a silent companion sat eating at the family table, his head bent over his plate, paying no heed to three pairs of eyes that saw nothing but him.

2

AFTER FOUR O'CLOCK

I SELDOM went off to play with the boys of the village, for up to that time, the year 189. ., I had suffered from a weakness of the knee which had left me timid and forlorn. I can still see myself trying to keep up with more nimble children, hopping on one leg . . .

So I was not often allowed to go out. I remember how Millie, who was very proud of me, would fetch me home, not sparing the smacks, when she came upon me hobbling about with a gang of street urchins.

The advent of Augustin Meaulnes, coinciding as it did with my recovery from this ailment, marked the beginning of a new life.

Before he came, when classes were over at four o'clock, an evening of solitude would stretch out before me. My father would carry the hot coals from the class-room stove to the dining-room fireplace; and one by one belated pupils would desert the chilling school-room where wisps of smoke still lingered. A few last games and capers out in the yard – then night. The two pupils whose turn it had been to sweep out the class-rooms would reach down their hooded capes from pegs under the playground roof and with their baskets hung over their arm race away, leaving the gate ajar . . .

Then, as long as a glimmer of daylight remained, I would go into the part of the building which comprised the Town Hall and sit tucked away in a corner of the Public Records office with its dead flies and flapping posters. I sat with a book on an old weighing-machine near a window overlooking the garden.

When night had set in, when the dogs in the neighbouring farmyard began to howl and a light showed through the window of our little kitchen I would go back. My mother was now seeing to preparations for supper. Mounting two or three steps of the stairway that led to the attic from the narrow kitchen, I would sit down without a word, my head pressed against the cold banisters, and watch her by the flickering light of a candle as she got her fire to draw.

But someone came and put an end to all these mild and childish pleasures. Someone blew out the candle which illumined for me the sweet maternal face bent over the evening meal. Someone extinguished the lamp around which we had been a happy family group at night-time when my father had closed all the wooden shutters. And that someone was Augustin Meaulnes, whom in no time the other boys began to call *le grand Meaulnes*.*

Once he became a boarder, in the first days of December, there was no further question of the school being deserted from four o'clock on. Despite the draughts let in by the banging door and the clatter of brooms and pails there were always a score of senior boys who stayed behind in the class-room, boys from the village and from the countryside, huddled around one central figure – Meaulnes. And then began endless discussions, interminable arguments, in which I ventured to take part too, half delighted, half uneasy.

As for Meaulnes, he hardly said a word, but it was for his benefit that every now and then one of the more loquacious lads would shove into the middle of the group, and calling on his mates one by one to bear him out, which they noisily did, would launch into some long tale of pillage while the others listened open-mouthed with silent laughter.

* No English adjective will convey all the shades of meaning that can be read into the simple word *grand* which takes on overtones as the story progresses. *Le grand Meaulnes* can mean the tall, the big, the protective, the almost-grown-up, even the great Meaulnes – or in schoolboy parlance, good old Meaulnes. But when the book has been put down, the phrase evokes in retrospect the image of someone not only tall or big but also daring, noble, tragic, fabulous. It is a phrase which has acquired a patina, for since its use as the title of a book which cast a spell over a whole generation of French readers, it enjoys the sort of nostalgic prestige, not untinged with affection, that one associates with familiar quotations.

Besides, would not *any* English adjective sound incongruous before a name which is pronounced like our word 'moan'?

The reader is therefore invited to accept the phrase in the original, leaving the context to supply the overtones. *Translator.*

Seated on a desk, swinging his legs, Meaulnes seemed to meditate. At appropriate moments he too would laugh, though charily, as if reserving his roars for some better story known only to himself. Then, as night came on and the rays from the windows no longer outlined the figures swarming round him, Meaulnes would heave himself up and make his way through the group, calling out, 'Come on now, off we go!'

And off they went. You could hear their cries well into the evening from the other end of the dark high street . . .

There were days now when I went along too. With Meaulnes I would stand at the doorway of the stables on the outskirts of the village when the farmers were milking their cows . . . Or we would step into a work-room, and from a dim recess the weaver's voice would be heard above the clatter of his loom singing out, 'Ah, here come the students!'

Usually by supper time we were nearing home again and might pause at the forge kept by Desnoues the wheelwright who was also a farrier. His premises had once been an inn, with a vast double doorway that was usually left open. From the street you could hear the sigh of the bellows and in the glare of the charcoal blaze you might see, amidst the wavering shadows and the clamour, country folk who had got down from their wagons for a chat, or perhaps another schoolboy who like us would be leaning against the doorpost staring in silence.

And it was there that it all began, about a week before Christmas.

3

'I USED TO TAKE A GREAT DELIGHT IN STANDING AT A BASKET-MAKER'S . . .'

IT had poured all day, letting up only towards evening. We had been bored to death. During recess no one had gone out. And every now and then my father, Monsieur Seurel, would call out, 'Now, now, boys – less noise please.'

After the last recreation period – the last 'quarter' as we called it – Monsieur Seurel who had been thoughtfully pacing stood still, rapped on a table with a ruler to quell the confused mutterings of a roomful of pupils at the end of their tether, and in the lull that followed flung out a question:

'Which one of you will drive to the station with François tomorrow to meet Monsieur and Madame Charpentier?'

They were my grandparents: Grandfather Charpentier, a retired forest-ranger, always clad in a long hooded cloak of grey wool and a cap of rabbit fur which, like an officer, he referred to as his *képi*. All the little boys knew him. In the morning, for his ablutions, he would draw a bucket from the well and splash about like the soldiers in days gone by, giving his tuft of beard a cursory dip. A ring of children, hands behind their back, would stand gaping, intrigued but respectful . . . They knew Grandmother Charpentier too, a little peasant woman in a knitted bonnet, for Millie made a point of introducing her into the junior class-room at least once during each annual visit.

Every year, shortly before Christmas, we drove to meet the train which arrived at two minutes past four. To get to us they had to travel across the whole breadth of the *Département* laden with bundles of chestnuts and Christmas fare wrapped in serviettes. Once they had crossed our threshold, both of them warmly swaddled, smiling, a little bashful, the doors were closed on them and a week of great festivity began . . .

It was thought prudent that someone go with me to help drive to the station, someone reliable who wouldn't upset us in the ditch and yet fairly good-natured, because Grandfather Charpentier would swear on slight provocation and my grandmother was somewhat talkative.

In response to Monsieur Seurel's question at least ten voices shouted in unison, '*Le grand Meaulnes! Le grand Meaulnes!*'

But Monsieur Seurel seemed not to have heard.

So they tried an alternative: '*Fromentin!*'

Still others: '*Jasmin Delouche!*'

The youngest of the Roy brothers, who galloped over the

fields mounted on a sow, called out in his piercing falsetto: 'Me! Me!'

Dutremblay and Mouchebœuf, more diffident, merely raised their hands.

I would have chosen Meaulnes; that would have transformed the jaunt in the donkey-cart into a great event. He too would have liked it, but he maintained a disdainful silence. By now all the older boys, like him, were perched on the forms, their feet on the benches, as always at times of special relaxation or rejoicing. Coffin, his smock pulled up and tucked into his belt, hugged the iron stanchion which supported the ceiling and started to shin up.

But Monsieur Seurel threw cold water on the assembly by announcing, 'That'll do, now. Mouchebœuf, you'll go.'

And everyone resumed his place in silence.

At four o'clock I was standing with Meaulnes in the icy yard streaked with rivulets left by the rain. Our eyes were turned towards the village where the glistening street was now drying under the assault of a squall. Presently young Coffin, his hood pulled over his head and a piece of bread in his hand, came out of his house and, hugging the wall, made off towards the wheelwright's where he paused at the doorway, whistling. Meaulnes pushed open the gate, called out to him, and soon all three of us were installed in the smithy, warm and glowing in spite of the glacial blasts that found their way in: Coffin and I seated near the forge, our muddy boots buried in a heap of white shavings; Meaulnes, his hands in his pockets, silent, leaning against the doorpost. Now and then some housewife coming from the butcher's would go by, head down into the wind, and we would glance up to see who it was.

No one spoke. The farrier and his mate, one hammering at a band of iron, the other working the bellows, flung tall shadows on the wall . . . I recall that evening as one of the great moments of my adolescence. I was filled with a happiness tinged with anxiety: I was afraid my companion would deprive me of the humble pleasure of driving to the station; at the same time, without daring to confess it to myself, I was counting on him for some extraordinary exploit that would be sure to turn everything upside down.

From time to time there would be a break in the steady peaceful rhythm of the work in the forge: a heavy ringing note as the smith let his hammer fall on the anvil. Holding close to his leather apron the band of metal which he had been shaping, he examined it, and then turning his eyes on us, as if to take a breather, called out, 'Well, young gents, how are things going?'

His mate, one hand still holding to the chain of the bellows, the other resting on his hip, looked at us with a broad smile on his face.

Then the heavy, noisy rhythm would be resumed.

During one of these pauses Millie went by, her scarf drawn tight against the wind, her arms full of small packages.

The smith asked: 'Will Monsieur Charpentier be coming soon?'

'Tomorrow. With my grandmother. By the four-two train. I'm going to meet them.'

'Taking Fromentin's carriage?'

Hastily I corrected him. 'No. Old Martin's.'

'I see! So you'll be gone quite a time!' Both he and his mate burst out laughing.

Then the latter, to keep the conversation going, remarked in his slow way, 'With Fromentin's mare you could have gone all the way to Vierzon . . . and picked them up there . . . They'll have an hour's wait there . . . It's only fifteen kilometres . . . You'd be back before old Martin got his donkey into the shafts!'

'Yes,' agreed the smith, 'that mare can certainly cover the ground . . .'

'And I dare say Fromentin wouldn't mind lending her.'

No more was said. Again the forge was a cave of sparks and clangour where each denizen kept his thoughts to himself.

But when it was time to leave and I got up to make Meaulnes a sign, he paid no attention. Leaning against the doorpost, his head thrust back, he seemed to be ruminating on what he had just been hearing. Seeing him like that, sunk in his own reflections, looking as if through leagues of fog at these tranquil workmen, I suddenly recollected a picture of Robinson Crusoe which portrayed him as a youth, before his long voyage, 'standing at a basket-maker's . . .'.

And I've often thought of it since.

4

THE FLIGHT

At one o'clock on the following afternoon the class-room of the upper form stands out clearly in a frozen landscape like a vessel at sea. The prevailing smell, however, is not one of lubricants and brine as on board a trawler, but an odour of fried herrings and scorched wool. The herrings had been fried on the top of the stove; the smell of cloth was caused by boys who, returning to school after lunch, had crowded too near the stove to get warm.

As the end of term is approaching, composition books have been distributed, and while Monsieur Seurel stands at the blackboard copying out the problems he has set us, a doubtful silence obtains, a silence ruffled by whispered exchanges or punctured by a stifled yelp and the beginning of a complaint voiced in the hope of intimidating an assailant:

'Monsieur! So-and-so is . . .'

As he writes down the problems, Monsieur Seurel is thinking of something else. Every little while he turns round and looks at us in a manner both vague and severe. The furtive ebullition subsides, only to bubble up a few seconds later, a simmer at first, gradually increasing to a boil.

Alone, in the midst of this agitation, I am quiet. Seated at the end of a row allotted to younger members of the class, near the high windows, I have only to lift my head a little to get a view of the garden, the brook that bounds it, and the fields beyond.

From time to time I stand on tiptoe and look away anxiously towards the farm of the Belle-Étoile. Meaulnes had not shown up after the noon break, and there was still no sign of him when classes resumed. His desk-mate must be as conscious of his absence as I am, but so far, engrossed in his composition, he has made no comment. Once he looks up from the page, the news will flash through the room and as sure as fate someone will give the alarm:

'Monsieur . . . Meaulnes . . .'

I know that Meaulnes has left – or, to be exact, I have a strong suspicion that he has decamped. Directly after lunch he must have leapt over the low wall and struck out across the fields towards the Belle-Étoile, crossing the brook at the Vieille-Planche. He will have asked for the loan of the mare to go and meet the Charpentiers. Perhaps even now they are putting her into harness.

The Belle-Étoile is over there beyond the brook on the hillside: a large farm hidden in summer by its elms and oaks and hedges. It faces a lane which leads one way to the station road, the other to the village. Surrounded by high greyish walls whose buttresses rise up from a moat of manure, this relic of feudal days is submerged by foliage in June, and on summer evenings the only signs of life that reach us are the rumbling of wains or the cries of a cow-herd. But today, from my window, between the trunks of bare trees I can see the wall of the farmyard, the gateway, and a bit farther on, through a gap in the hedgerow, a section of the frosty lane which skirts the brook and leads to the station road.

Nothing is stirring as yet in this bright winter scene. As yet there is no change.

Monsieur Seurel writes down the last word of the second problem. He usually sets three. What if, for once, he should only give out two? . . . In that case he will at any moment return to his table overlooking the room and discover that Meaulnes is not in his place. He will send two boys off to scour the village and they will be sure to trace him before the mare is ready . . .

Monsieur Seurel, still at the blackboard, is giving his arm a rest . . . And now, to my great relief, he starts a new paragraph:

'This one,' he remarks, 'is mere child's play.'

Two short black poles which projected beyond the wall of the Belle-Étoile and which can only have been the shafts of a carriage have disappeared from view. That means that preparations for Meaulnes's departure are now under way. And now there is the mare herself, her head and shoulders advancing between the posts of the gateway. Now she is standing – no doubt an extra bench is being fitted into the back of the carriole for the passengers Meaulnes is supposed to be meeting. At last the whole turn-out moves slowly away from the farmyard, disappears for a moment behind the hedgerow, and proceeds at the same slow pace as far as the section of the lane I can see through a gap in the hedge. And in the black figure holding the reins, one arm resting negligently, peasant fashion, against the side of the vehicle, I recognize my companion Augustin Meaulnes.

Again everything is hidden by the hedge. But two men who have been standing in the gateway watching the carriage move off, are now looking at one another as if in doubt, their uneasiness visibly increasing. At length one of them, making a megaphone of his hands, shouts out to Meaulnes, follows him down the lane, runs a few steps . . . Meanwhile, the carriage having come slowly on to the main road and presumably now out of sight from the lane, there is a brusque change in the driver's bearing. He is on his feet, like a Roman charioteer, one leg thrust forward. Shaking the reins with both hands, he urges the mare on at full speed, and in no time they are over the brow of the hill. Back in the lane, the man who had called after Meaulnes has again broken into a run. The other is racing across the fields in our direction.

A few minutes later, as Monsieur Seurel turns away from the blackboard brushing chalk dust from his fingers, just as three voices at the back of the room are calling out, 'Monsieur! *Le grand Meaulnes* has gone . . .' the farmer has reached the door and pushes it wide open. He is wearing a blue smock. Taking off his hat, he stands on the threshold:

'Excuse me, Monsieur, was it you gave that big chap leave to ask for my carriole . . . to go to Vierzon . . . to meet your relations? . . . we began to wonder . . .'

'Certainly not!' Monsieur Seurel interrupts.

At once the class is in an uproar. The three boys nearest the exit make a bound for the door; it is they whose privilege it is to fling stones at the pigs and goats that sometimes invade the garden to nibble at silver-leaved plants in the flower-bed. We hear their hobnailed sabots pounding over the flagstones of the school and then, more faintly, crunching the gravel and skidding as they veer into the road through the little gate. Most of the boys are fighting for a place at the windows over-looking the garden; others stand on the forms peering over their heads . . .

Too late. *Le grand Meaulnes* has got clean away.

Monsieur Seurel is speaking to me. 'You'll go to the station all the same, with Mouchebœuf. Meaulnes doesn't know his way to Vierzon. At the cross-roads he may take a wrong turning and be too late for the train.'

Millie has thrust her head through the doorway of the other class-room.

'What in the world is going on?'

Outside in the street people are collecting in knots. The farmer stands there, stolid and stubborn, his hat in his hand, like someone pleading for justice.

5

THE CARRIAGE RETURNS

I HAD met my grandparents at the station, and after dinner when they were seated before the fire telling us all that had happened to them since the last holidays I found my attention wandering.

The little gate of the courtyard was quite close to the dining-room. It had a way of creaking when you opened it. Usually, at the beginning of our long country evenings, I was secretly listening for that grating noise. It would be followed by the sound of sabots on the gravel or on the boot-scraper, sometimes by the lowered voices of visitors putting their heads together before venturing to come in. Then a knock. A neighbour, the village schoolmistresses – someone come to break the monotony of the winter evening.

Tonight, for once, I had no need of outside distractions, since all those I loved were here in the house; and yet I was on the alert for every slightest sound in the outer darkness, waiting for the door to open.

The old man sat there looking like some shaggy shepherd of Gascony, his feet heavily planted in front of him, his stick between his legs, his shoulder bending as he knocked his pipe against the sole of his boot. His kind and watery eyes would turn with approval on my grandmother as she chattered away about their journey, their neighbours, their hens, or tenants behind with the rent . . . I was among them, but absent.

I imagined the approach of a carriole which would be drawing up at the gateway. Meaulnes would jump down and come in as if nothing had happened . . . Or, more likely, he would first take the mare back to the Belle-Étoile; but I should soon be hearing his step on the road and the creaking of the gate . . .

But I heard nothing.

Grandfather was now staring into space, his eyelids growing heavy as sleep overcame him. Grandmother, a trifle put out, had to repeat something she had just said, something which had gone unheeded:

'Is it that boy that's worrying you?' she finally asked.

For at the station I had questioned her anxiously. During the halt at Vierzon she had seen no one in the least like my description of *le grand Meaulnes*. So he must have been delayed on the road. His bold attempt had failed. And on the way home I had nursed my disappointment while Grandmother talked to Mouchebœuf. On the glazed road sparrows swirled away from the hoofs of the trotting donkey. Now and then the frozen stillness of the afternoon was pierced by the distant call of a shepherdess or the voice of some country lad hailing a comrade across the clearing between two fir-groves. And whenever I heard that long-drawn-out cry from the desolate hillside a shudder went through me, for it might almost have been the far-away voice of my companion bidding me follow him . . .

All this was still going round in my brain when it was time to go to bed. Grandfather had already retired into the red room – it was really the parlour and still damp and raw from having been shut up since the previous winter. Before making him free of the apartment my mother had removed the lace head-rests from the arm-chairs, taken up the rugs, and placed the more fragile ornaments in a place of safety. He had put down his stick, thrust his boots under a chair, and blown out his candle. The rest of us were standing about, saying good night before going off to our rooms, when we were arrested by the sound of wheels.

It sounded like two vehicles, one following the other at a very slow trot. Then the pace slackened, and presently there was a halt just under the dining-room window which overlooked the road but which was blocked.

Picking up the lamp, my father went towards the door which had already been locked for the night. He went out, pushed open the gate, and stood on the steps holding the lamp high over his head, the better to see.

There were, in fact, two carriages, the horse drawing the second being hitched to the one in front. A man had got down and stood looking around him . . .

'Is this the Town Hall?' he inquired, coming nearer. 'Where can I find Monsieur Fromentin, a farmer – address, the Belle-Étoile? I found his horse wandering down a lane without a driver – near the road to Saint-Loup-des-Bois. With my lantern I was able to make out the name on the plate of the carriage. As it happened to be on my way I took it in tow, to avoid accidents. But it's made me terribly late all the same.'

We stood there stupefied. My father went closer, examining the carriole by the light of the lamp.

'Whoever was in it left no trace – not even a horse blanket. The mare is tired; she's limping a bit . . .'

I had pushed forward and was staring at this conveyance that had gone astray and come back to us like a piece of wreckage brought in by the tide – the first, and for all I knew the last debris of the adventure on which Meaulnes had launched himself.

'Is it far to this Fromentin's?' the stranger was asking. 'If it is, I'll leave the carriage with you. I've lost too much time already – at home they'll be worried.'

My father agreed, all the more so as we could return the mare at once without having to explain what had happened. Later we could decide what to tell the neighbours and what to write to Madame Meaulnes . . . So the stranger flicked his whip and drove away, declining the drink we offered him.

We left my father to drive over to the farm and went silently indoors. From the depths of his room, where he had relit the candle, Grandfather called out:

'What is it? The wanderer come back?'

The two women exchanged a glance.

'Yes. He's been to see his mother. Go back to sleep. There's nothing to worry about.'

'Glad to hear it. It's just as I thought.'

His mind at rest, he turned over in bed and went to sleep.

It was the explanation we gave to the village people. As for the fugitive's mother, it was decided to wait a while before writing to her. So for three long days we kept our worries to ourselves. I still see my father, back from the farm towards eleven, his moustache damp from the night air, talking it over with Millie, his voice kept low but vibrant with wrath and distress . . .

6

A TAP ON THE WINDOW

THE fourth day was one of the coldest of the winter. Early
in the morning the first boys to arrive in the yard kept warm
by making a slide around the well. Once the fire was lit in the
school-room stove they would make a rush for it.

Just inside the gateway some of us kept a look-out for the
boys who lived in outlying districts. They would come in
dazzled from their tramp over acres of hoar-frost with reports
of thick ice on the ponds and of hares scampering out of the
thickets. Their smocks were permeated with the odours of
stable and hayloft which gave a strong flavour to the air of
the class-room once they were crowded round the glowing
stove. On that particular morning, one of them produced from
his basket a frozen squirrel he'd picked up on his way to school.
I remember him lifting out the stiff little animal and trying to
hang it by its feet to a post under the playground roof . .

Then the sluggish winter morning lessons began . . .

A sudden tap on the window-pane made us look up. And
there, through the glass of the door, we saw *le grand Meaulnes*
shaking the rime from his smock. His head was held high, and
in his eyes there was a look of exultation.

The two boys nearest the door scrambled up to open it.
Then in the doorway a sort of secret conference took place.
At length the truant decided to enter the room.

The gust of cold air coming in from the empty yard with *le
grand Meaulnes*, the wisps of straw clinging to his clothes, but
above all the impression he gave of a traveller exhausted,
famished, but under a spell – it set us tingling with an odd
feeling of pleasure and curiosity.

Monsieur Seurel stepped down from the platform where he
had been giving us dictation, and Meaulnes walked towards
him with something aggressive in his attitude. I recall thinking
how fine my tall companion looked at that moment in spite of

30

his fatigue and his bloodshot eyes – the result, no doubt, of nights spent in the open.

He went straight to the master's desk and said with the assurance of someone delivering a message:

'I've come back, Monsieur.'

'So I see,' said Monsieur Seurel, surveying him in wonderment. 'Go to your desk and sit down.'

The young man turned and came towards us, his shoulders slightly hunched, smiling with the mocking air of seniors who have incurred punishment. Grasping the edge of his desk he let himself down on the bench.

'I'll give you a book,' said Monsieur Seurel. Every head in the room was still turned in Meaulnes's direction. 'You can be studying it while your class-mates go on with their dictation.'

The class settled down again. Now and then *le grand Meaulnes* glanced towards me, or looked out of the window through which one could see the garden as white as cotton, all life arrested, and fields abandoned except for an occasional crow. In the class-room the red stove gave out an oppressive heat. His elbows on the desk, his head in his hands, my comrade was trying to read. Twice I saw his eyes close and I thought he was falling asleep.

At last, half raising his hand, he said, 'I'd like to lie down, Monsieur. I haven't slept for three nights . . .'

'You may go,' said Monsieur Seurel, only too anxious to avoid a scene.

With heads lifted, pens in mid-air, and feelings of regret we watched him go, his boots all muddy, the back of his smock badly creased . . .

What a long morning it was! Towards noon we heard our traveller stirring in the attic-room overhead, getting ready to come downstairs. At lunch time I came upon him in front of the dining-room fire, seated near my grandparents who felt somewhat constrained. On the curtains a shadow ballet was being performed as pupils tall and short capered past, let loose into the snowy yard on the stroke of twelve.

All I recall of that meal is that no one said a word and

31

everyone was embarrassed. There was a chill over everything: the oilcloth under the plates, the wine in the glasses, the red tiles on which our feet rested. Lest the runaway be goaded into open revolt, it was decided that he should not be questioned. And he took advantage of this truce by remaining silent.

When at last dessert was finished, we two escaped into the courtyard; the playground at midday, with snow turning to slush under stout sabots, with ice turning to waterfalls at the edge of the roof, a place of games and shrieks and yells. Meaulnes and I ran along close to the buildings. Two or three of our village friends catching sight of us dropped their game and came running with whoops of joy, hands in their pockets, scarves flapping, sabots squirting up mud. But my companion darted into the big school-room, me at his heels, and shut the door-window just in time to stem the horde of pursuers. A violent shindy ensued, window-panes rattling, sabots clattering, a concerted shove against the door that threatened to bend the iron uprights – but Meaulnes, at the risk of cutting his finger on its jagged ring, had turned the key in the lock.

Such behaviour used to annoy us very much. In the summer boys shut out like this would hare round through the garden and sometimes get in by a window before one had time to close them all. But it was now December and all the windows were fastened. Outside, the besiegers made a few pushes against the door, there was a brief hail of abuse, then one by one they made off, adjusting their mufflers.

In the class-room, which now smelt of chestnuts and vinegary wine, two monitors were shifting the desks. To fill in time before the afternoon session I lolled about near the stove. Meaulnes was searching the desks, including the master's until at last he found what he wanted: a small atlas. He began to study it with a passionate intensity, standing on the platform, his elbows on the desk, his head in his hands.

I was about to go over to him; I would have put a hand on his shoulder and no doubt together we would have traced out the route he had taken, when suddenly the door communicating with the other class-room burst open, and in came Jasmin Delouche with a shout of triumph, followed by three country boys and a lad from the village. One of the windows of the other class-room must have been left half open and they had got in that way.

Jasmin Delouche, though rather small, was one of the oldest pupils of the upper form. He was extremely jealous of Meaulnes, although he pretended to be his friend. Before our boarder's advent Jasmin had been cock of the walk. He had a pale, rather insipid face, and sleeked-down hair. The only son of a widow who kept an inn, he played the man and was for ever showing off by repeating things he had heard the clients say over a game of billiards or a glass of vermouth.

Meaulnes looked up, scowled as the invaders elbowed their way towards the stove, and called out:

'Can't you ever leave people in peace for five minutes?'

'If you don't like it,' said Jasmin, 'you should have stayed where you were.' His eyes were averted, but he was emboldened by the presence of a bodyguard.

I think Augustin had reached the stage of fatigue where rage takes possession before you have time to master it. He had turned pale.

'That's enough from you,' he said, straightening up and shutting his book. 'Out you go!'

Jasmin sneered:

'Oh? Just because you managed to stay away for three days you imagine you're the boss around here now!'

And, to draw the others into it:

'It would take more than you to put us out.'

But Meaulnes had already pounced. In the scuffle sleeves were torn, seams ripped away. Of the boys who had come in with Jasmin, only one, Martin, intervened.

'Let him alone,' he shouted, his nostrils distended, shaking his head like a ram.

With a brutal shove Meaulnes sent him staggering backwards, his arms beating the air. Then, seizing Delouche by the collar with one hand, opening the door with the other, he tried to fling him out. But Jasmin clung to the desks, his hobnailed boots scraping over the flagstones as he dragged his feet. Meanwhile Martin had recovered his balance and was approaching warily, with lowered head and fury in his eyes. Meaulnes released Delouche to grapple with this lout and might have found himself in a tight corner if at that moment a door leading to the kitchen had not opened. There stood Monsieur Seurel, glancing over his shoulder, still speaking to someone out of sight . . .

Hostilities ceased at once. Those who had contrived to keep out of the fight stood sheepishly round the stove. Meaulnes, his sleeves gaping at the shoulders, went off to his desk. As for Jasmin, his voice could be heard during the few moments left before the stroke of the ruler announcing the resumption of lessons, as with flushed cheeks he cried out:

'He's getting too big for his boots . . . Thinks himself clever . . . As if we didn't know where he'd been!'

'Idiot!' said Meaulnes when complete silence had once more fallen. 'I don't even know myself.'

And with a shrug he settled down to learn his lessons.

7

THE SILK WAISTCOAT

WE slept in a big garret, half bedroom, half attic. Other rooms provided for assistant masters had regular windows; no one knew why ours had only a dormer. The door scraped the floor and would not shut properly. When we went upstairs at night, shielding the candle from the draughts that pervaded the big house, we would try again to close the door and again have to give up the attempt. And all through the night we could feel, like a presence, the silence that overflowed the three lofts and came creeping into our room.

It was here, at the end of that winter's day, that we were together at last, Augustin and I.

My clothes were off in a jiffy and heaped on a chair by my bed – an iron bed with curtains of cretonne patterned with vine-leaves. But my companion, taciturn, was taking his time. From my bed I watched his movements. He would sit for a few moments on the edge of his low uncurtained cot, then get up to pace the room, taking his things off as he walked to and fro. And as he moved about the room, the candle he had placed on a small wicker table made by the gipsies threw on the wall a gigantic shadow that never came to rest.

Unlike me, he was careful of his schoolboy garments, folding and setting them in order with a sort of sad concentration, absent-minded but methodical. I can still see him laying his heavy belt across the seat of a chair, folding his extremely rumpled and soiled black smock over the chair-back, taking off the dark-blue jacket he wore under his smock and then, turning his back and bending over, spreading the jacket across the foot of his bed . . . But when he straightened up and faced me again, I saw that instead of the little brass-buttoned waistcoat which went with our school outfit, he had on a strange one of silk, cut very open, and fastened by a row of small and closely set buttons of mother-of-pearl.

It was quaint, and it was charming, like something that might have been worn by the young men who danced with our grandmothers in the eighteen-thirties.

I can see now the tall countrified schoolboy, bareheaded – for he had carefully placed his cap on top of his other garments – his face so young, so brave, and yet already so stern. He was pacing again as he began to undo this mysterious item of a costume that did not belong to him. And it was odd to see him, in shirt-sleeves, wearing trousers he had already outgrown and boots caked with mud, fingering a waistcoat that had been tailored for a marquis.

The touch of the silk startled him out of his reverie, and he glanced at me as if with an uneasy conscience. It made me want to laugh. He smiled when I did, his face lighting up.

That gave me courage to question him. 'Do, please, tell me,' I whispered. 'What is it? Where did you find it?'

His smile went out like a snuffed candle. He passed his heavy hand over his close-cropped head once or twice, then, as if unable to hold out any longer against his desire, he picked up his jacket, put it on, buttoned it over the delicate waistcoat, slipped on his rumpled smock – and then wavered, giving me

35

a sidelong glance . . . In the end he sat down on his bed, drew off his boots and let them fall noisily to the floor, and like a soldier on outpost duty fully dressed for emergency, he stretched himself out on the cot and blew out the light.

In the middle of the night I woke up with a start. Meaulnes was standing with his cap on, groping about for something hanging on a peg: a cape, which he threw over his shoulders . . . The room was in darkness; even the dim light sometimes reflected by the snow was lacking. A black and bitter wind blew through the dead garden and sent gusts against the roof.

I raised myself on one elbow and spoke in a whisper:

'Meaulnes! Are you going away again?'

He made no reply. Then, seized with a sort of frenzy, I said:

'Very well! I'm going too. You've got to take me with you.' And I jumped out of bed.

He came over, took me by the arm, and sat me down again.

'No, François, I can't take you with me. If I were sure of the road I'd let you come. But first I've got to find it on the map. So far I haven't been able to.'

'Well in that case you can't go back yourself!'

'It's true,' he said with an air of dejection. 'It's all so pointless . . . Come on, now, get back into bed. I promise not to leave without you.'

He began to pace the room again, back and forth. I didn't dare say anything more. He would stop, and then be off again, walking faster, like someone rummaging about in his memory, sorting out scraps, matching them against each other, comparing, calculating, suddenly glimpsing a clue, losing it before it is within reach, having to begin all over . . .

That was not the only night when, wakened around one o'clock by the sound of footsteps, I saw him pacing through the bedroom and the lofts – like those sailors who can never shake off the habit of keeping watch and in the heart of some Breton retreat get up and dress at regular intervals to inspect an earthly horizon.

Two or three times during January and the first half of February I was thus roused from sleep. Le grand Meaulnes stood there with all his clothes on, the big cape over his shoulders, ready to go. Yet each time, on the threshold of that mysterious domain into which he had strayed once already, he stood hesitant. About to raise the latch of the door to the stairs and leave by the kitchen door, which he could easily have opened without anyone hearing, he again drew back . . . Then through the long hours of the night he paced the floor of the empty rooms, brooding and feverish.

At last one night – around the middle of February – it was he himself who woke me, his hand gently pressed on my shoulder.

It had been a day full of tumult. Meaulnes, who had lost all interest in the games of his former comrades, spent the last recreation period seated at his desk, absorbed in a small atlas of the *Département*, the Cher, calculating distances, his finger tracing a course on the page while he sketched out on a sheet of paper some mysterious itinerary. All around him there was a clatter of sabots; boys kept racing in and out, leaping over benches, chasing one another from desk to desk . . . They knew it was risky to jostle Meaulnes when he was trying to concentrate, but towards the end of the recess two or three of the village lads, as though acting on a dare, came up on tiptoe and looked over his shoulder. Then one of them nerved himself to give the others a push that flung them against Meaulnes. In a flash he had shut the atlas, concealed his notes, and reached for the nearest intruder while the others made off.

It happened to be Giraudat, a surly fellow who began at once to whine and kick but was promptly ejected from the room, though not before he had had time to shout out in his rage:

'You big bully! No wonder they're all against you. No wonder they're going to make war on you . . .'

. . . and a string of insults to which we replied without really understanding what he was talking about. It was I who shouted the loudest, for I had taken Meaulnes's part. There was now a sort of pact between us. His promise to take me away with him, and the fact that he had never said, as the others were for ever saying, that I was not 'game', had bound me to

37

him for life. And I never stopped thinking about his mysterious expedition. I had come to the conclusion that he had met some girl or other. She was sure to be far more beautiful than any of the local girls, prettier than Jeanne whom we used to see in the convent garden through a keyhole in the gate; or than Madeleine, the baker's daughter, so pink and so blonde; or Jenny up at the château who was beautiful but mad and never allowed out. There could be no doubt that it was a girl he was thinking about, at night, like the hero of a novel. And I had made up my mind to ask him about her, bravely, the next time he woke me up. . . .

On the evening of this latest scuffle, after school, the two of us were in the garden collecting tools, picks and shovels which had been used during the day, when we heard battle cries on the road. It was a band of young rowdies marching in step four abreast, like a well-drilled company, led by Delouche, Daniel, Giraudat, and a fourth we didn't know. They caught sight of us and began hooting in unison. So the whole village was against us, and some military game was being played from which we were excluded.

Tranquilly Meaulnes walked over to the shelter to put away the spade and mattock he had been carrying on one shoulder . . .

But at midnight I felt his hand on my arm, and woke up with a start.

'Get up,' he whispered. 'We're leaving.'

'Do you know the way now?'

'A good part of it . . . The rest,' he said grimly, 'we'll have to find out as we go along.'

I sat up in my bed. 'Look, Meaulnes – listen to me. There's only one thing to do, and that's for us to go exploring by daylight, using your map, till we locate the part of the route still missing.'

'Yes, but that part is such a long way off!'

'Very well, we'll drive there, in the summer, as soon as the days get longer.'

A long silence that followed could only mean that he agreed.

At last I said: 'As we're both going to look for the girl you've fallen in love with, Meaulnes, you might at least let me know who she is. Tell me about her.'

He sat down on the foot of my bed. In the darkness I could just make out his bowed head, his folded arms, his knees. Then he took a deep breath, like someone whose heart was too full and who could no longer keep the secret to himself . . .

8

THE ADVENTURE

BUT that night my companion did not tell me everything that had happened to him on the road. And even when he did decide to take me fully into his confidence, during days of sorrow I shall come back to, it remained for a long while the great secret of our adolescence. But now that it is all over, now that nothing is left but the dust of

So much that was evil, so much that was good

there is no reason why the strange story should not be told.

At half past one on the bitterly cold afternoon when he set out for Vierzon, Meaulnes drove along at a good speed, knowing he had not left himself too much time. At first, in his glee, all he could think of was the surprise in store for us when he came back at four with my grandparents. For at that moment this was certainly his only objective.

Then, as the cold began to numb him, he wrapped his legs in the blanket which he had declined but which the men at the Belle-Étoile had insisted on his taking.

By two o'clock he was rattling through the village of La Motte. He had never passed through a village during school hours and was amused by the sleepy and deserted aspect of its only street. Here and there a curtain would move and a woman's head appear for an instant, but that was all.

When he had traversed the village, leaving the school-house behind, he had a choice of two turnings. He hesitated. He knew vaguely that to get to Vierzon one must bear to the left – but there was no one to ask. So he pushed on at a steady gait down a road which turned out to be narrow and badly surfaced. For a while he skirted a wood of firs and at length met a carter to whom he shouted out an inquiry. But the mare was pulling hard and kept trotting. The carter may not have understood the question. At any rate he made a vague reply with a gesture no less vague, and Meaulnes decided to take a chance on the road he was on.

Then once more he was surrounded by a vast frozen plain devoid of landmarks: no living thing in sight but now and then a magpie which rose in alarm and flapped away to perch on the stump of an elm. Wrapping the heavy blanket around him like a cape, the traveller now stretched out his legs and, leaning against the side of the carriole, fell into a sleep that must have lasted for some time . . .

. . . When at length, chilled through in spite of the blanket, he came to his senses, the scene was transformed. It was no longer a landscape of distant horizons merging into a boundless white sky, but a patchwork of fields, still green, behind high enclosures. On either side were ditches in which water was flowing beneath the ice. Everything pointed to the proximity of a river. And between the hedgerows the road was now merely a rough narrow lane.

The mare had left off her jog-trot some distance back. Meaulnes used his whip, but nothing would induce her to move faster than a slow walk. Then, leaning forward, his hands on the dashboard, he bent down and discovered that she was limping – something wrong with one of her hind legs. He drew up and got down in some alarm, muttering to himself:

'We'll never get to Vierzon in time for that train.'

He hardly dared acknowledge the most alarming thought of all: that he might have lost his way, that the road he was on might not be the road leading to his destination.

He made a careful examination but could find no sign of

injury. Flinching whenever he touched her hoof, the mare would lift it, then paw the ground with her heavy, clumsy shoe. It was now obvious that she had picked up a pebble. Used to dealing with animals, Meaulnes sat down on his heels and tried to take the hoof in his right hand and wedge it between his knees, but the carriage got in his way. Twice the mare eluded him and moved a few yards farther on. Meaulnes was struck on the side of the head by the step of the vehicle and even more painfully on the knee by a wheel. But he persevered and finally succeeded in reassuring the timorous animal. But the stone was so deeply embedded that he was obliged to use his knife to work it free.

When at last he was able to straighten up, half dizzy, his vision blurred, he was appalled to find that night was already falling . . .

Anyone but Meaulnes would have turned back. Only by doing so could he hope to avoid going still farther astray. But he reflected that he must already be a long distance from La Motte. And while he slept it was quite possible that the mare had turned into a cross-road. In any case this lane must lead sooner or later to a village . . . Add to all these reasons the fact that this headstrong youth, as he climbed back into his seat while the impatient horse began pulling on the reins, felt mounting within him a frantic desire to achieve something and get somewhere in spite of all obstacles.

As he cracked his whip the mare shied, then broke into a brisk trot. The darkness was rapidly increasing. In the rutted lane there was now barely room for the carriage to pass between the hedgerows. Now and then a dead branch would catch the spokes of a wheel and break off with a snap . . . When night had closed in, Meaulnes suddenly thought, with a twinge, of the dining-room at Sainte-Agathe where at that moment we must all be gathered round the table. Then a surge of anger overwhelmed him, soon followed by a feeling of self-congratulation, for there was something exhilarating in the thought of having broken loose like this without in the least meaning to . . .

9

A HALT

WITHOUT warning the mare slowed down as if she had stumbled on something unexpected. In the dark Meaulnes could just see her neck bending down, her head jerking up again; then she stood, head down as if sniffing. He heard a sound of gurgling water, and saw that the lane was cut off by a brook. Fordable no doubt in summer, the current was now so strong that ice had been unable to form; to attempt a crossing was risky.

He reined in, backed a short distance, then stood up, completely at a loss. It was then that he descried through the branches a faint glimmer of light. It was not far away: over there beyond two or three meadows . . .

He got down and seized the bridle, leading the mare still farther back, talking to her soothingly as she nervously jerked her head in the air:

'Now then, now then, old girl! We're nearly there. We'll soon find out where we are.'

He saw an aperture in the hedge, and a half-open gate. He led the horse through into a small meadow, his feet sinking into lush grass, the carriage jolting along behind. His head against the animal's cheek, he could feel her warmth and the heaving motions of her breathing . . . He took her to the edge of the paddock, threw the blanket over her, and then, separating the branches of the hedge that bounded it, once more located the light. It came from a house that stood out in isolation.

There were, however, still three meadows to cross, and a treacherous brooklet through which he was obliged to wade . . . At last, jumping down from an embankment, he found himself in the yard of a cottage. Somewhere a pig was grunting. At the sound of footsteps on the frozen ground a dog set up a furious barking.

The shutter over the door was open and Meaulnes could

see that the light which had guided him came from a log fire, for no other light was showing in the house. A woman got up and came to the door without any trace of fear. A clock with suspended weights struck half past seven.

'Excuse me,' he said. 'I'm afraid I trod on your chrysanthemums.'

She stood there for a moment, looking at him, holding a basin in her hand.

'It is pretty dark out there,' she agreed. 'Can't see where you're going.'

He stepped across the threshold and stood for a moment glancing around the room: at the walls covered like those of an inn with pictures from illustrated papers, at the table on which he noticed a man's hat.

'Isn't your husband at home?' he asked, taking a seat.

'He'll be back in a minute.' And, reassured, she added, 'He's just gone out to fetch some logs.'

'Not that I wanted him particularly,' said Meaulnes, drawing his chair closer to the fireplace. 'It's just that a party of us are out looking for game. I wondered if you could spare us a little bread.'

For *le grand Meaulnes* was well aware that among country folk, and especially on a lonely farm, it was prudent to feel one's way forward and above all not to give the impression of being a stranger to the district.

'Bread!' she exclaimed. 'I'm afraid we haven't much to give you. The baker calls every Tuesday but for some reason he didn't show up today.'

Augustin, who had been hoping there might be a village within easy reach, was disconcerted.

'The baker from where?'

'Why, the baker from Vieux-Nançay,' she replied as if that went without saying.

'Just how far do you reckon it is from here to Vieux-Nançay,' he inquired, trying to conceal his anxiety.

'By road I couldn't rightly say. But cross-country it's three and a half leagues.'

And she began to tell him about her daughter who was in

43

service there and came on foot to see her the first Sunday of every month. The people she worked for . . .

Meaulnes, now utterly at sea, broke in:

'You mean to say there's no place nearer to you than Vieux-Nançay!'

'Well of course there's Les Landes. That's only five kilometres. But it has no shops or bakery – only a small fair once a year, on Saint Martin's day.'

Meaulnes had never heard of Les Landes. He was so wildly off his course that he almost found it funny. But the woman, busy at the sink washing her basin, inquisitive in her turn, now looked at him directly and said rather deliberately:

'Then perhaps you don't belong to these parts . . .'

At this moment an old man came in with an armful of wood which he threw down on the flagstones. In a loud voice, as though he were deaf, the woman explained what the young man wanted.

'Well,' he said simply, 'it should be easy . . . But draw up your chair, Monsieur. You're not getting the heat.'

A few minutes later they were both sitting close to the andirons: the old man breaking faggots to throw on the blaze, Meaulnes provided with bread and a bowl of milk. Happy to find himself in this humble cottage after so much anxiety, at the end – so he thought – of his queer adventure, the rover was already planning to come back one day with his friends to revisit these good people. He didn't know that this was a mere halt, that his wanderings would soon be resumed.

Presently he asked to be put on the road to La Motte. And growing a little more truthful, he said he and his carriole had got separated from the other sportsmen and he was in fact quite lost.

At this both his hosts were so insistent that he spend the night there and wait till morning before turning homewards, that Meaulnes ended by accepting their offer and got up to see about stabling the mare.

'Mind the holes in the path,' the old man warned him.

Meaulnes dared not confess that he hadn't come by the

'path'. He thought of asking the friendly old man to accompany him. For a moment he stood on the threshold, wavering. The difficulty of coming to a decision almost made him reel. Then he stepped out into the dark farmyard.

10

THE SHEEPFOLD

To get his bearings he climbed the little slope from which he had leapt into the yard.

Slowly and with difficulty as before, he made his way back by grassy banks and through barriers of willow towards the corner of the paddock where he had left the carriole. But it was no longer there ... Motionless, with throbbing temples, he strained to identify all the sounds of the night, expecting at any moment to hear the faint jingling of harness near at hand. But there was no sound ... He scoured the meadow and came to the gate. It was partly open but half lying on the ground as if a cart wheel had gone over it. The mare had evidently gone off that way by herself.

Coming out in the lane he walked a few yards and caught his foot in the blanket, which must have slipped off the mare's back. It was at least an indication of the direction she had taken. He began to run.

With no other thought than a wild determination to catch up with the carriole, his heart pounding, urged on by an impulse between panic and fear, he kept running ... Now and then he stumbled over ruts. In the total darkness he missed turnings and, too tired to check his impetus, would plunge into a hedge, falling down on the thorns, scratching the hands he held out to protect his face. Now and then he would stop, listen, and go on again. At one moment he thought he heard the sound of a vehicle; but it was only a tumbrel jolting over a road far away to the left ...

By now his knee, injured by the wheel of the carriage, was causing him such pain that he had to give up the pursuit. His leg had grown stiff. He told himself that unless the mare had gone off at a gallop he would by this time have overtaken her. Besides, a horse and carriage could never just vanish: sooner or later someone must find it. So he turned and began to retrace his steps, exhausted, wrathful, and lame.

At length he seemed to be back in the surroundings he had so recently left and before long he caught a glimpse of the light he was looking for. An opening in the hedge revealed a sunken pathway.

'That must be the path the old man referred to,' thought Augustin.

And he turned into it, glad to have no more hedges and banks to get over. After a little way the path began to deviate to the left, and the light seemed to be swerving in the opposite direction. Arriving at a point where two paths met, in his haste to get back to the modest refuge, he mechanically followed the one which seemed to lead directly towards it. But he had hardly taken a dozen steps when the light disappeared, either because it was hidden by a hedge or because the old folk, tired of waiting for him, had closed their shutters. Taking a chance, he made straight across the fields for the spot where he had last seen the light. Then, after climbing over one more fence, he found himself on still another path . . .

Thus, little by little, the trail became a maze, and the one thread that attached him to those he had left was broken.

Disheartened, worn out, he decided despairingly to follow the path he was on till the end. After walking some twenty or thirty yards he emerged into a broad grey meadow where he could make out, at wide intervals, deeper shadows that must be juniper bushes, and there, in a depression, a building of some sort. He plodded on towards it. It seemed to be a large pen for livestock, possibly an abandoned sheepfold. The door of the shed yielded, opening with a groan. The light of the moon, when the wind swept the clouds away, came through chinks in the wall. A mouldy smell pervaded the place.

With nothing better to be hoped for, Meaulnes lay down on the damp straw, propped on one elbow, his head in his hand. At last, taking off his belt, he drew up his knees and snuggled as best he could into his smock. He thought with longing of the blanket he had left on the roadside and was by now so cross with himself, so utterly wretched, that he was ready to cry . . .

So he forced himself to think of something more cheerful. Chilled to the marrow, he recalled a dream, or rather a vision, of his childhood which he had never confided to a soul. One morning, instead of waking up in his bedroom where his coats and trousers were hanging, he was in a long green apartment with curtains the colour of foliage. The room was bathed in a light so sweet he felt one should be able to taste it. Close to the nearest window a girl sat sewing; he could only see her back. She seemed to be waiting for him to waken . . . Too inert to slip out of bed and explore this enchanted dwelling, he sank back into sleep . . . But next time, he vowed, he would get up. Perhaps the very next morning . . .

II

THE MYSTERIOUS DOMAIN *

AT daybreak he set out again. But his knee had swollen and was hurting him. So sharp indeed was the pain that he was forced to stop and rest every few minutes. In the whole of the Sologne it would have been hard to find a more desolate spot than the region in which he now found himself. Throughout the morning he saw no one but a shepherdess guiding her

---

* *Domaine* is another portmanteau word for which it would be hard to find an English equivalent. 'Country estate' has inappropriate connotations. 'Demesne' fits in some ways but is a word not commonly in use. To the characters in the story *domaine* would be an everyday word suggesting a fairly important private property attached to a manor house or château; at the same time it could have the broader, vaguer meaning usually associated with our use of the word 'domain'. The author in fact does use it repeatedly with this less precise, more poetical meaning in mind. With these qualifications a literal, if not exact, translation seems the best solution. *Translator.*

flock some distance away. He called out, and attempted to run; but she disappeared without having heard him.

He limped on in the direction she had taken but his progress was dishearteningly slow . . . Not a roof, not a living soul, not even the cry of a curlew from the reeds of the marshes. And over all this desolation streamed the thin and frigid light of a December sun.

It must have been getting on for three in the afternoon when at last he saw the spire of a turret above a large grove of fir trees.

'Some forsaken old manor,' he surmised. 'Some deserted pigeon-house . . .'

But he kept wearily to his course. At a corner of the wood he came upon two white posts marking the entrance to an avenue. He turned into it and had not gone far when he was brought to a halt in surprise and stood there, stirred by an emotion he could not have defined. Then he pushed on with the same dragging steps. His lips were cracked by the wind which at moments almost took his breath away. And yet he was now sustained by an extraordinary sense of well-being, an almost intoxicating serenity, by the certitude that the goal was in sight, that he had nothing but happiness to look forward to. It reminded him of days gone by when he would nearly faint with delight on the eve of the midsummer fête, when out in the village street they would be setting up fir trees and his bedroom window was obstructed by branches.

Then he scoffed at himself for rejoicing at the prospect of 'a tumble-down pigeon-house full of owls and draughts . . .'

Disgruntled, he paused, half inclined to turn back and walk on till he came to a village. As he stood trying to make up his mind, his eyes fixed on the ground, he noticed that the avenue had been swept in wide symmetrical circles, as on very special occasions at home. It was like the high street of La Ferté on the morning of Assumption . . . He could not have been more surprised had he come upon a group of holiday-makers stirring up a cloud of dust as if it were June . . .

'And yet,' he mused, 'of all places for a fête – this wilderness!'

On nearing the first bend in the avenue he caught a sound

of voices. Stepping aside in haste, he squeezed through the bushy saplings, stooped down out of sight, and held his breath. The voices sounded very young – and indeed a group of children now passed, quite close to him. He couldn't catch all they were saying, but one of them – it sounded like a little girl – spoke with such an air of weight and assurance that Meaulnes smiled to himself . . .

'Only one thing bothers me,' she was saying. 'And that's the question of horses. Take Daniel: we'll never be able to prevent him from riding the big yellow pony . . .'

A young boy's mocking voice interrupted. 'Of course you can't prevent me. They've given us *carte blanche*, haven't they! Even to break our necks if we want to . . .'

The voices died away just as another group approached.

'Tomorrow morning,' a little girl was saying, 'if the ice is broken, we're going to make a boat trip.'

'But will they let us?'

'You know very well we're planning the party to suit ourselves.'

'Yes, but if Frantz were to get here tonight with his fiancée . . .'

'Suppose he does! He'll agree to whatever we say.'

'So there's going to be a wedding,' Augustin concluded. 'But is this place run by children? . . . What a very strange domain!'

He was tempted to leave his hiding-place and ask where he could get something to eat and drink. He straightened up, and saw the second group of children walking away: three little girls in straight frocks that just reached their knees. They wore pretty hats tied with ribbon, a white feather curling down at the back. One of them, half turning towards her companion, listened while the latter embarked on a complicated explanation, marking her points with a finger in the air.

'I should only frighten them,' thought Meaulnes, with a rueful glance at his torn smock and the uncouth belt that was part of his uniform as a pupil at Sainte-Agathe.

To avoid meeting the children on their return up the

avenue, he cut across through the trees in the direction of the 'pigeon-house', not too sure what to ask for when he got there. He came to the edge of the wood and found it bounded by a low mossy wall. Beyond it, between the wall and some outbuildings, there was a long narrow courtyard crammed with carriages – like an inn-yard on the day of the local fair. He saw vehicles of every size and shape, their shafts in the air: stylish little carriages with room for four; wagonettes with cross-benches; old-fashioned coaches with ornamental sides and railings; antiquated Berlins whose windows were up.

Hidden behind the trees and taking care not to be seen, Meaulnes was studying this scene of confusion when he noticed in one of the annexes on the far side of the courtyard a half-open window just above the driver's seat of a wagonette. Two iron rods, like those one sees across the permanently closed shutters of stable buildings, must once have barred this opening, but time had worn them loose.

'I'll get in that way,' he decided. 'I'll sleep in the hay, and leave first thing in the morning without having frightened any pretty little girls.'

He got over the wall with difficulty on account of his injured knee, and passing from carriage to carriage, from the bench of a wagonette to the roof of a Berlin, he came level with the window, and gave it a push. It swung open noiselessly.

He found himself not in a hayloft but in a very large low-ceilinged apartment that was evidently a bedroom. In the winter twilight he could see that the table, the mantelshelf, and even the arm-chairs were cluttered with tall vases, expensive objects of every description, and old weapons. One end of the room was cut off by hangings which no doubt concealed an alcove.

Meaulnes had closed the window, partly because of the cold, partly for fear of being seen from outside. He crossed the room, drew aside the hangings, and discovered a broad low bed heaped with old books in gilt bindings, lutes with broken strings, candelabra – all thrown down pell-mell. Pushing everything into a corner of the alcove he lay down to rest and sort out the elements of this strange adventure into which he had plunged.

Deep silence brooded over this domain. Only the muffled wailing of the December wind could at intervals be heard.

And lying here relaxed, Meaulnes began to wonder whether, in spite of his odd encounters, in spite of the voices of the children in the avenue and the concourse of carriages, he was not after all in some old barn of a place left to its fate in the winter solitude.

But before long he fancied that the wind had caught up some strains of lost music which it was bringing to his ears. It evoked memories at once charming and sad. He recalled days when his mother, still young, sat at the piano in the late afternoon while he, behind a door opening on the garden, sat listening till it grew dark, never saying a word . . .

Was someone really playing the piano here – now ? . . .

The question in his mind remained unanswered, for weariness was overcoming him and he soon fell asleep.

12

WELLINGTON'S ROOM

IT was night when he woke up. Numb with cold he turned over first on one side, then on the other, creasing and rucking up his smock. A dim light filtered through the hangings of the alcove.

Sitting up on the bed, he thrust his head cautiously between the curtains. The window had been opened, and two green Chinese lanterns hung in the embrasure.

Scarcely had he taken this in when he became aware of steps on the landing and voices carrying on a conversation in undertones. He drew back into the alcove, his hobnailed boot knocking against one of the bronze objects he had shoved against the wall. For a moment he held his breath in trepidation. The steps drew nearer, and two shadows stole into the room.

'Don't make a noise,' said one.

'All the same,' said the other, 'it's about time he woke up.'

'Have you stocked his room?'

'Of course – just like the others.'

A shutter banged in the wind.

'You didn't even have the sense to shut the window. Now the wind has blown out one of the lanterns, and you'll have to light it again.'

'Why?' argued his mate in an access of sloth and dejection. 'What's the point of showing a light on a mere stretch of country – a desert as you might say? Who's going to see it?'

'Who's going to see it? Why, some of them will still be on their way here after dark. Out there on the road in their carriages they'll be very glad to see a light.'

Meaulnes heard someone strike a match. The man who had last spoken and who seemed to be the leader went on in a drawling voice – the voice of a Shakespearian grave-digger:

'I see you've put green lanterns in Wellington's room. Any particular reason why they shouldn't be red ones? . . . You don't know any more about it than I do.'

A pause, and then:

'This Wellington – an American, wasn't he? Now, is green an American colour? You should know. You're an actor. You've travelled.'

'Travelled!' exclaimed the 'actor'. 'Oh yes, I've travelled. But I haven't seen much. You can't see much in a caravan.'

Meaulnes peeked through the curtains.

The leader of the two was a big man, bare-headed, enveloped in an enormous top-coat. He sat with crossed legs holding a long pole to which a number of coloured lanterns were attached, and tranquilly watched his mate at work.

As for the actor, no one could have been less prepossessing. Tall, thin, shivering, with dull shifty eyes, several teeth missing, and a draggling moustache – he had the look of a drowned man stretched out on a slab. He was in shirt-sleeves and his teeth chattered. That he had no better opinion of his person than anyone else was implied in his voice and his gestures.

He stood in thought for a moment, an expression of wry humour on his face, then went towards his mate, arms spread out as if opening the deepest recesses of his heart:

'If you want my opinion . . . I can't see why they round up scum like us for this kind of fête. It doesn't make sense, mate . . .'

Unmoved by this outburst of humility, the big man, his legs still crossed, watched the other finish his task, yawned, sniffed placidly, then, with his pole over his shoulder, got up and walked away, saying as he went:

'Come on, now. Time to dress for dinner.'

The actor followed him but paused at the alcove where he made a ceremonious bow and began in a tone of bland mockery:

'Mister Sleepy-head, may I remind you it's time to rise and dress up as a marquis, even if you're only a pauper like myself. Then you're to go down and join the fancy-dress party, that being the good pleasure of the little ladies and gentlemen.'

In the accents of a side-show hawker he added:

'Our comrade Maloyau, affected to the kitchen service, will appear in the role of Harlequin. The immortal Pierrot will be impersonated by your humble servant.'

And with a final bow he departed.

13

THE STRANGE FÊTE

As soon as they had gone, Meaulnes emerged from his refuge. His feet were stone-cold, his limbs were stiff, but he was rested and the pain had left his knee.

To go down to dinner – nothing would suit him better. 'I'll just be a guest whose name no one can remember. Besides, I'm not really an intruder: it's quite obvious that Monsieur Maloyau and his friend were expecting me . . .'

After the complete darkness of the alcove he was able to see fairly well by the light of the green lanterns. The vagabond had indeed 'stocked' his room. Cloaks hung from pegs on the wall. On a heavy dressing-table with a cracked marble top he saw the wherewithal to transform any lad who had spent the night in an abandoned sheepfold into a fop. On the mantel there was a tall torch and matches to light it with. But the floor had not been waxed and his boots trod on patches of grit and plaster. Once again he had the impression of being in a house long since abandoned . . . Moving towards the fire-place he nearly stumbled over a pile of cartons and small boxes. He lit a candle and peered under their lids.

He saw costumes designed for gallants of a bygone era: frock-coats with high velvet collars, smart low-cut waistcoats, long white neckcloths, and patent-leather shoes in the fashion of the early years of the century. He didn't dare touch them, but when he had had a wash, shivering the while, he took down one of the great cloaks and put it on over his school-boy's smock, drawing close the pleated cape-collar. Exchanging his hobnailed boots for a pair of pumps, but bare-headed, he was ready to go downstairs.

Descending a wooden staircase without meeting anyone, he came out into a corner of a dark courtyard. A blast of cold night air smote his cheek and lifted a flap of his cloak.

He took a few steps and looked around him. There was just enough light in the sky to enable him to get his bearings. He was in a small court surrounded by outhouses. Everything looked old and derelict. Doors had long since been removed from the lower entrance to the stairways. Missing window-panes left black holes in the walls. And yet the whole scene had a mysterious air of festivity. Coloured reflections came out from low rooms where no doubt lanterns had also been placed, in windows overlooking the countryside. The ground had been cleared of rank weeds and swept. As he stood there he thought he could hear singing – the voices sounded juvenile and came from somewhere beyond this confused huddle of buildings where the wind shook the branches silhouetted against a pattern of pink, green, and blue window-spaces.

He was standing still, in his great cloak, leaning forward

slightly like a sportsman, the better to hear, when an incredible youth stepped out from an adjoining building which looked quite uninhabited.

He was wearing a top-hat with curved brim which shone in the darkness like silver; a frock-coat with collar pushing up into his hair; an open waistcoat; and trousers with foot-straps . . . This young dandy, who could not have been over fifteen, came springing along as though his elastic foot-straps gave him an extra bounce and passed by in a flash, making Meaulnes a deep mechanical bow without stopping, and disappeared in the darkness in the direction of the main building: farm, château, abbey, whatever it might be, whose turret had guided the lost schoolboy in the early afternoon.

After a moment's hesitation Meaulnes set off in the wake of this odd little personage. They crossed a wide space, half court, half garden, proceeded down a path bordered with shrubbery, turned round a fenced-in fishpond, went past a well, and arrived at last before the entrance to the house.

A heavy wooden door, arched at the top and studded like the door of a presbytery, stood ajar. The young dandy went in. Meaulnes followed and had scarcely taken a step in the hall before finding himself in the midst of laughter, song, shouts, and scamperings, though there was no one in sight.

At the far end of this hall there was a corridor at right angles. He was trying to decide between exploring it and opening one of the doors behind which he heard voices, when he saw two girls running down the corridor, one chasing the other. On tiptoe in his fine pumps he ran forward to see and catch up with them. A sound of doors opening, a glimpse of two fifteen-year-old faces flushed by the sharp night air and the keenness of the pursuit, faces framed in tall Directoire hats tied under the chin, about to vanish in a great blare of light. For one moment they pirouette, their wide skirts swirling and billowing, revealing the lace of quaint pantalettes; and then, their performance finished, they dart into a room and close the door behind them.

Meaulnes stood still in the dim hallway, dazzled, reeling, feeling now very much of an intruder – with his hesitant, awkward appearance he might easily be taken for a thief! He made up his mind to turn back when once more he heard steps at the end of the passage and the sound of childish voices. Two small boys were coming towards him.

Assuming an air of self-possession, he asked:

'Isn't it nearly time for dinner?'

The older boy replied. 'Come with us. We'll show you the way.'

And in the trusting, friendly way of children on the eve of an important feast-day, they took him by the hand, one on either side. He guessed them to be the children of peasants dressed in their best: breeches reaching half-way below the knee, revealing coarse woollen stockings and tiny clogs; jerkins of blue velvet, caps to match, and white neckties.

'Do you know her?' the older boy asked his comrade, an urchin with a round head and candid eyes.

'No, but my mother said she had a black dress and a muslin collar and looked like a pretty pierrot.'

'Who does?' asked Meaulnes.

'Why, Frantz's fiancée, of course . . . that he's gone to fetch . . .'

Before Meaulnes could ask anything more they reached the door of a large room with a low ceiling, where a great fire was blazing. Tables made from planks set on trestles were spread with white cloths, and around them was seated a very mixed gathering of people, dining in style.

14

THE STRANGE FÊTE

CONTINUED

IT was the sort of meal which on the night before a country wedding is served to relations who have come a long way to attend the celebrations.

The two boys dropped Meaulnes's hand and ran off to an adjoining room from which came childish shouts and a clatter of spoons. Boldly, and quite self-composed, Meaulnes stepped over a bench and sat down beside two old peasant women. Ravenous, he began to eat without ceremony, and it was some time before he lifted his head to take stock of his table companions and listen to what they were saying.

For that matter there was little conversation. The guests seemed hardly to know one another. They must have come from distant towns or remote parts of the country. Here and there at wide intervals along the tables were bewhiskered old men, and others, clean-shaven, who looked as if they had once followed the sea. They were flanked by other old men who in many ways resembled them: the same tanned skin, the same keen eyes under bushy brows, the same neckties as narrow as shoe-laces . . . But it was easy to see that these latter had never navigated beyond the confines of their own canton and that if they had pitched and tossed in many a gale and many a downpour, it was during voyages perhaps as rough but certainly less fraught with peril, as they steered their ploughs across the fields and back again . . . There were not many women among them: a few old bodies with faces like wizened apples under frilled bonnets.

There was no one there with whom Meaulnes did not feel safe and at ease. Later he explained this impression in these words: 'When you've done something quite inexcusable, you try to ease your conscience by telling yourself that someone, somewhere would forgive you. You think of old people, perhaps indulgent grandparents, who are convinced beforehand that whatever you do is all right.' And certainly the good people sitting at these tables belonged in that category. As for the rest, they were adolescents, or children . . .

Meanwhile the women beside him had begun to chat.

'At the earliest,' said the older of the two in an odd high-pitched voice which she tried in vain to soften, 'the young man and his fiancée can't get here before three tomorrow afternoon.'

'How you talk!' said the other, 'If you go on you'll make me lose my temper.' But under her knitted bonnet she looked placid enough.

'Then work it out for yourself,' the older woman retorted, quite unperturbed. 'An hour and a half in the train from Bourges to Vierzon. Seven leagues by road from Vierzon to here . . .'

And the argument went on. Meaulnes did not miss a word. Thanks to this peaceable little quarrel he began to get a glimmer of enlightenment. Frantz de Galais, the son of the house – a student or a sailor, possibly a midshipman, it wasn't quite clear – had gone to Bourges to fetch the girl he was to marry. Strange as it might seem, this lad, for he must be extremely young as well as capricious, ordered the affairs of the domain to suit his own whims. One of these was that the château should look like a palace *en fête* when his fiancée arrived. And to welcome her he himself had invited all these children and mild old folk . . . These were the few facts that emerged from the chatter of the two women; all the rest remained shrouded in mystery as they got back on the subject of the probable hour of the young people's arrival. One said next morning, the other said next afternoon.

'My poor Moinelle' – it was the younger, less excitable one who was speaking – 'you're as scatter-brained as ever.'

'And you as stubborn as ever, my poor Adèle,' came the peaceful retort with a shrug of the shoulders. 'It's four years since I last saw you and you haven't changed a bit.'

And they went on bickering without the slightest trace of ill humour.

Eager to learn more, Meaulnes at last intervened.

'Is his fiancée as pretty as they say?'

They looked at him as if not knowing how to reply. No one but Frantz had seen the girl. He, on his way home from Toulon, had stopped off in Bourges and come upon her one evening in great distress in one of the gardens there known as the 'fens'. Her father, a weaver, had turned her out of doors. She was very pretty, and there and then Frantz had decided to marry her. It was a strange story; but hadn't Monsieur de Galais, his father, granted all his wishes, and his sister Yvonne as well! . . .

Meaulnes was feeling his way towards further inquiries

when a charming couple appeared in the doorway: a girl of sixteen in a velvet bodice and flounced skirt, and a young man in a coat with a high collar and trousers with foot-straps. They danced their way across the room; others followed them; then more came running, screaming, chased by a tall pierrot with whitened face in trailing sleeves, wearing a black cap, his toothless mouth stretched in a grin. He ran with long clumsy strides, half leaping, waving his empty sleeves. The girls seemed a little afraid of him, but the young men shook hands with him, while the younger children, thrilled, ran after him with piercing cries. As he went by, his dull eyes rested on Meaulnes, who detected under this now clean-shaven mask Monsieur Maloyau's mate, the mountebank who had hung up the lanterns.

The meal was finished and the guests got up from the table.

In the passages groups were forming for round dances and farandoles. Somewhere strings were playing a minuet . . . Meaulnes, his head half buried in the collar of his cloak which stood out like a ruff, was losing all sense of identity. Infected by the gaiety he too joined in the pursuit of the pierrot through corridors which were now like the wings of a theatre where the spectacle has spilled over from the stage. And well into the night he was lost in the throng taking part in a joyous masquerade. He would open a door and find that a magic-lantern show was in progress, with children loudly clapping their hands . . . Or in a salon crowded with dancers he would get into conversation with some young fop and pick up hints about the costumes to be worn on the ensuing days . . .

In the end, constrained by such an excess of merriment, dreading that someone might notice his schoolboy garb under his cloak, he sought refuge in a more dimly lit part of the house where nothing was to be heard but the subdued sound of a piano.

Opening a door he found himself in a dining-room lit by a hanging lamp. Here all was quiet, but here too a party was in progress: the participants were infants.

Some of them, seated on foot-stools, held albums on their

laps; others, kneeling on the floor, were arranging an exhibition of pictures on a chair in front of them; the rest, grouped round the fire, said nothing, did nothing, but were content to listen to the faint sounds of revelry that echoed through the big house.

A piano was being played in an adjacent room. The door stood open, and out of curiosity Meaulnes went over to see who it was. He stood looking into a small drawing-room. A young woman, or possibly a mere girl – her back was turned – a reddish-brown cloak over her shoulders, was playing softly some simple familiar airs or part songs. On a sofa near the piano six or seven small boys and girls sat as primly as children in a picture, listening and 'being good' as children are when it is getting very late, though now and then one of them, propping himself up with his wrists, would slide down and go into the dining-room, whereupon another child, having seen all the picture-books, would come in and take his place ...

After gambols which, however amusing, had been hectic and a little mad, when even he had joined in a wild chase after the leaping pierrot, Meaulnes was now immersed in a deep and wonderfully peaceful contentment.

Without making a sound, while the girl continued to play, he went back into the dining-room and sat down, reached for one of the red albums scattered about on the table, and began to turn the pages absent-mindedly.

A small boy left his place on the floor, plucked at his sleeve, and climbed on his knee to see what he was looking at. In a moment he was joined by a playmate who took possession of the other knee. And Meaulnes began dreaming in a way that recalled his old dream. His imagination lingered over the illusion that he was in his own house one fine evening, a married man, and that the unknown but charming person playing the piano in the next room was his wife ...

15

THE MEETING

NEXT morning Meaulnes was one of the first to be ready. Acting on the advice he had received, he had put on a simple black suit with a close-fitting coat, the sleeves puffed at the shoulder, a double-breasted waistcoat, trousers so wide at the feet that they almost hid his fine shoes – and a top-hat.

The courtyard was still empty when he went down, and as he stepped into it, it was as if he had been wafted away into a morning of spring. It was in fact the mildest morning of that winter, with sunlight reminding one of the first days of April. The frost was thawing and the damp grass glistened as if moistened with dew. In the trees small birds were twittering and the breeze against his cheeks was soft.

Like guests up and about before their host, he moved aimlessly into the court half expecting to hear some friendly cheerful voice call out:

'What, you up already, Augustin?'

But for some time he wandered alone through the court and the garden. Looking away towards the windows and the turret of the main building he could see nothing astir, though both panels of the heavy rounded door stood open. High above it the first rays of the sun blazed out on one of the upper windows as if this were the early morning of a summer's day.

It was the first time he had seen the interior of the grounds by daylight. The courtyard had recently been sanded and raked. A half-demolished wall separated it from the garden. One end of the outbuildings in which his own room was situated was occupied by stables, an odd jumble of structures smothered in vines and invaded by bushes run wild. The whole domain was hedged in by the woods which concealed it from the low-lying countryside except towards the east where one could see blue hills covered with rocks and still more fir trees.

Roaming through the garden, he came upon the fishpond and peered over the rickety fence which surrounded it. The pool was still edged with ice, thin and lacy like foam. He caught sight of himself in the water, as if he were bending over the sky. And in the figure dressed in the clothes of a romantic student he saw another Meaulnes: not the collegian who had made off in a farmer's carriole, but a charming and fabulous creature out of a book, a book one might receive as a prize . . .

He hurried towards the main building, for he was getting hungry. In the big room where he had dined a woman laid a place for him. He sat down and she at once poured coffee into one of the bowls lined up on the tablecloth.

'You're the first one down, Monsieur.'

He hesitated to speak, because he was still afraid he might suddenly give himself away as an intruder. But he must find out when they would be leaving for the boat trip he had heard about.

'Not for another half hour, Monsieur. No one else is down yet.'

So he went out again to wander round the house, looking for some sign of a landing-stage. The long building had the proportions of a château, though its two wings, unequal in size, gave it something of the look of a church. He went round the south wing and suddenly had before him a landscape of reeds as far as the eye could see. The marsh water at this point came to the foot of the walls, and at the doors small wooden balconies were suspended above the lapping wavelets.

For some time he strolled along the shore over a sandy stretch that resembled a towpath, stopping here and there to stare up at tall dusty windows through which apartments in a state of dilapidation could be dimly seen, or lumber-rooms cluttered up with wheelbarrows, rusty tools, and broken flower-pots, when all at once he heard footsteps on the sand.

It was two women, one old and bent, the other young, fair, and slender. Her inconspicuous clothes, simple but charming, after all the fancy costumes of the night before, struck him at first as extraordinary.

They paused for a moment to look about them and Meaulnes, in a hasty conclusion that later seemed to him wildly wide of the mark, told himself:

'Probably one of those girls they call eccentric – perhaps an actress they've got here for the fête.'

Meanwhile the two women passed close to him, and he stood watching the girl. Often afterwards, when he had gone to sleep after trying desperately to recapture that beautiful image, he saw in his dreams a procession of young women who resembled her. One wore a hat like hers; one leaned slightly forward as she did; one had her innocent expression, another her slim waist, another her blue eyes – but not one of them was this tall slender girl.

He had time to notice a head of luxuriant fair hair and a face with small features so delicate as to be almost over-sensitive. Then she was moving away from him and he noticed the clothes she was wearing which were as simple and modest as garments could possibly be . . .

Irresolute, wondering whether he dare accompany them, he heard the girl say to her companion, as she turned slightly towards him:

'The boat ought to be here at any moment now . . .'

And Meaulnes followed them.

The old lady, though feeble and shaky, did most of the talking which she sprinkled with laughter, the girl making gentle replies. And the same gentleness was in the look, innocent and serious, which she turned on him as the two women walked down towards a landing-stage: a look which seemed to say:

'Who are you? How do you happen to be here? I don't know you . . . And yet I do seem to know you.'

Other guests were now standing about under the trees. Then three pleasure-boats came alongside to take on the passengers. One by one young men doffed their hats and young ladies bowed at the approach of the two women, who seemed to be the lady of the château and her daughter. It was all very strange – the morning itself, the excursion . . . In spite of the sun there was a chill in the air and the women drew more tightly about their throats the feather boas which were then in fashion . . .

The old lady stayed behind on the shore, and without knowing how it happened, Meaulnes found himself on board the same little vessel as the young lady of the house. He leaned against a rail, one hand protecting his hat from the high wind, unable to take his eyes from the girl, who had found a seat in a sheltered part of the deck. She looked at him too. She would answer the remarks of her neighbours with a smile, then her blue eyes would rest on him gently. He noticed that she had a habit of biting her lip.

In deep silence they drew away from the shore. Nothing could be heard but the purr of the engine and the wash from the bows. It might have been a morning of midsummer. They might have been bound for some country estate where this girl would saunter under a white sunshade, doves cooing through the long afternoon . . . But an icy gust of wind brought a sharp reminder of December to the people taking part in this strange fête.

They went ashore at a point wooded with firs. On the landing-stage the passengers, pressed close to one another, had to wait till a boatman unlocked the padlock of the barrier . . . In the days that followed, Meaulnes was never to recall without a surge of emotion that moment on the shore of the lake when the face that was soon to be lost to him was there, so close to him – that pure profile on which his eyes lingered until they were ready to fill with tears. And he remembered noticing on her cheek, like a delicate secret she was confiding in him, a trace of powder . . .

And now, on shore, everything fell into place as in a dream. While children ran about shouting and laughing, and their elders broke up into groups and moved away through the woods, Meaulnes kept to the path where the girl was walking only a few steps ahead. He came up with her before he had given himself time to reflect and said simply:

'You are beautiful.'

But she hurried on without replying and turned into a side-path.

Young people darted through the paths, played games, or wandered wherever their fancy guided them. The young man bitterly reproached himself for what he called his bad manners, his boorishness, his stupidity. He walked aimlessly on, convinced that he would never again set eyes on that lovely creature, when there she was, coming towards him. The path was narrow and she would have to pass close. With ungloved hands she was drawing back the folds of her long cloak. He noticed her low black shoes, and her ankles, so slender that at moments they seemed to bend and one feared to see them break.

This time the young man bowed, and said in a low voice: 'Will you forgive me?'

'I forgive you,' she said gravely. 'But I must get back to the children; it's they who are giving orders today. Good-bye.'

Augustin begged her to stay for a moment. His manner was awkward but in his voice there was so much perturbation that she listened, and walked along more slowly.

'I don't even know who you are,' she said at length.

To each word she gave the same stress, except for the last one which she spoke more gently . . . Then her face resumed its calm expression, her blue eyes focused on some object far away, her teeth pressing her lip.

'Nor do I know your name,' said Meaulnes.

The path brought them into open country, and some distance ahead guests were converging on a small house that stood in complete isolation.

'That's Frantz's house,' she said. 'I must leave you . . .'

She hesitated, looked at him for a moment, then said with a smile:

'My name? . . . I'm Mademoiselle Yvonne de Galais.'

And then she was gone.

No one was living in what they called 'Frantz's house' but Meaulnes found it filled from roof to cellar with festive invaders. He had no opportunity to explore his surroundings, for haste was being made to eat the cold lunch which had been brought up from the boats – not the most appropriate sort of meal for the season, but apparently what the children had decreed. Then it was time to turn back.

As Mademoiselle de Galais was leaving the house, Meaulnes

went towards her, and taking up the conversation where she had dropped it, said:

'The name I gave you was a more beautiful one.'

'Really? And what was it?' Her face remained grave.

But thinking he might have blundered again, he kept it to himself.

'Mine is Augustin Meaulnes. I'm a student.'

And for a few moments they talked in a leisurely way, with enjoyment, like friends. Then there was a change in the girl's manner. Less distant now, and less grave, she seemed more uneasy. It was as if she dreaded what Meaulnes might be going to say and recoiled in advance. She was quivering at his side, like a swallow which had come to rest for an instant but was already trembling with the wish to resume its flight.

And when he began to speak of his hopes she replied, gently:

'But what's the use? . . . What's the use?'

And yet when at last he summoned up courage to ask permission to return one day to this wonderful domain, she said quite naturally:

'I shall be expecting you.'

They came in sight of the landing-stage. She stood still a moment, then said pensively:

'We're both children. We've been foolish. We must not go back in the same boat. Good-bye – don't follow me.'

Disconcerted, Meaulnes stood and watched her move away. A little later, when he too had reached the shore, he saw her turn, before losing herself in the distant throng, to look back at him. For the first time her eyes rested on him in a steady regard. Was it meant as a final farewell? Was she forbidding him to accompany her? Or was there perhaps something more she would have liked to say? . . .

As soon as the guests returned to the manor the pony races took place in a broad sloping meadow behind the home farm. This was to be the last item in the day's programme. It had been assumed that the young couple would arrive in good time for these races, over which Frantz himself would preside.

But they had to begin without him. Boys dressed as jockeys

66

were leading up frisky beribboned ponies; girls in riding habits were provided with older and more docile mounts. The shouts and the juvenile laughter, the wagers and the bell-ringing, gave one the impression of being wafted away and set down on the velvety turf of a miniature race-course.

Meaulnes recognized Daniel and the little girls with a white feather in their hats whom he had heard the previous afternoon when approaching the house . . . But most of the spectacle was lost to him as he looked everywhere for another hat, one trimmed with roses, and a reddish-brown cloak. But Mademoiselle de Galais did not appear. He was still searching when a final volley of bell-ringing signalled the end of the racing. Amidst a burst of cheers a small girl on an old white mare had come in first. She rode past in triumph, the plumes of her hat streaming out behind her.

Then stillness settled down over the scene. The games were ended and Frantz had not appeared. No one seemed to know what to do next. There were embarrassed consultations. At last, in twos and threes, the guests went back to their rooms to await in silent constraint the arrival of the young host and his fiancée.

16

FRANTZ DE GALAIS

THE racing had ended too soon. It was half past four and still daylight when Meaulnes got back to his room, his head swimming with the events of his extraordinary day. He sat down at the table. There was nothing to do until it was time for dinner and the celebrations that were to follow.

Meanwhile the wind had got up and was now as strong as on the previous night. It would swirl round the house with the roar of a torrent, or break into the hissing stridency of a cascade. Now and then the iron blower rattled before the grate-front.

For the first time Meaulnes felt the slight depression that

follows a day which has been almost too perfect. He thought of making a fire, but when he tried to raise the blower he found it had rusted solidly into place. He began to roam about, putting the room in order. He hung up his fine raiment, stood the cluttered chairs against the wall, and made the place tidy as if for a prolonged sojourn.

Aware none the less that he might have to leave without warning, he carefully folded his own schoolboy clothes over the back of a chair, as if they were his travelling costume, and tucked his boots beneath it: they were still caked with mud.

Then, feeling more at ease, he sat down and surveyed this new home which he had put in order.

Now and again the window overlooking the carriage yard and the wood beyond was spattered with rain-drops. Relaxed, now that he had tidied up his room, he had begun to feel perfectly happy. Here he was, a mysterious tall youth, a stranger among strangers, in a room he had made his own. He had obtained more than he could ever have dared hope for. And merely to recall the face of a girl in the high wind turning to look at him gave him all the happiness he needed at the moment . . .

Lost in a daydream, he scarcely noticed that night had fallen, and it was dark before he even thought of lighting one of the torches. A rush of cold air blew open a door communicating with a room which, like his own, overlooked the carriage yard. Getting up to close it, he saw that there was a light in the room. He approached, and put his head through the half-open door. By the light of a candle on the table he could see someone pacing the floor, someone who must have got in by the window, which was wide open. As far as he could make out it was a very young man. Hatless, a travelling cape over his shoulders, he walked ceaselessly back and forth as if distracted by some intolerable pain. The draught from the window ruffled the folds of his cape, and whenever he approached the table the candle-light picked out the gilt buttons of his finely tailored frock-coat.

He was whistling something between his teeth: the tune of

a ditty sung by sailors, and the girls they meet in their taverns, to cheer themselves up.

The agitated pacing was suddenly broken off, and the youth leaned over the table, opened a box, and took out some sheets of paper . . . Meaulnes could now see his profile clearly in the candle-light: delicate aquiline features, without moustache, thick hair parted on the side. He had stopped whistling. Extremely pale, his lips parted, he seemed at the very end of his strength, as if he had been struck to the heart.

Meaulnes stood there in two minds: should he be discreet and withdraw? Or should he go forward, put a friendly hand on the young man's shoulder, and say something? . . . Then the young man himself looked up, stared for a moment, and without any sign of surprise came forward and in a tone which he tried to keep steady said:

'I don't know you, Monsieur. But I'm not sorry to see you. Since you're there, I may as well explain to you . . . It's like this . . .'

But he seemed to have lost his way. When he had said 'It's like this . . .' he had grasped the lapel of Meaulnes's coat, as though to fix his attention. Then he looked away towards the window, as if trying to put his thoughts in order. Meaulnes saw him blink his eyes and guessed that he was finding it hard to hold back the tears.

Then, swallowing his grief at a gulp, like a child, and without turning his eyes from the window, he went on in an altered voice:

'What I was going to say is this: it's all over; the fête is ended. You may tell them so when you go down. I've come home alone. My fiancée will not be coming. Whether from scruples, or timidity, or lack of faith . . . Let me try to explain, Monsieur . . .'

But he was unable to go on. His face was working. And he did not explain. Turning brusquely away, he crossed to the shadowy depths of the room where he began opening and closing drawers filled with clothing and books.

'I must get ready to leave. I don't want anyone to disturb me.'

He brought various objects to the table: a toilet case, a pistol . . .

Greatly disturbed, Meaulnes turned and walked away without daring to say a word or offer his hand in parting.

Downstairs it was already apparent that the company had guessed there was something amiss. Most of the girls had changed into everyday clothes. In the main building dinner had begun, but in an atmosphere of confusion: guests were eating in haste, like travellers with no time to lose.

There was a continuous coming and going up-and-down-stairs and back and forth between this dining-room-kitchen and the stables. Those who had finished their meal stood about exchanging good-byes.

Meaulnes turned to a country lad who was hurrying to finish his dinner, his felt hat on his head and a serviette tucked into his waistcoat. 'What's happening?' he asked.

'We're leaving . . . It was decided all of a sudden. We were all standing around, left to ourselves. We'd waited till the last minute. It was five. No chance of their turning up then. So somebody said: suppose we clear out . . . So everybody got ready to go.'

Meaulnes said nothing. He had no further reason for remaining. Hadn't he reached the end of his adventure? Hadn't he obtained all he could hope for – at least for the present? For that matter he had hardly had time to learn by heart the wonderful things that had been said that morning. For the moment there was nothing to stay for. Soon he would come back – this time without any false pretences . . .

'If you want to come with us,' said his new acquaintance, who was a lad of his own age, 'you'd better get your things on quick. We'll be harnessing in a few minutes.'

Leaving his meal half eaten, Meaulnes went pounding off without telling any of the guests what he knew. The park, the garden, the courtyard were now blotted out. And tonight there were no lanterns in the windows. But since this meal was after all the concluding feast in what should have been a wedding celebration, some of the more uncouth visitors, no

doubt spurred on by wine, had burst into song. And as he
made his way back Meaulnes heard vulgar songs desecrating
a park which for two days had harboured much grace and
many marvels. It was a portent of disintegration. He passed
the fishpond where that morning he had studied his reflection.
How everything had changed since then! . . . He had left the
rowdy chorus behind but could still hear snatches of song:

> Dear little libertine, where have you been?
> Your bonnet's awry,
> Your hair's coming down . . .

And again:

> I've got on red shoes . . .
> Lover, good-bye!
> I've got on red shoes . . .
> For ever, good-bye!

On reaching the stairway leading to his isolated room he
collided in the dark with someone coming down, who said:
'Good-bye, Monsieur.'

And, wrapping his cape round his shoulders as if he were
chilled, he disappeared. It was Frantz de Galais.

The candle which Frantz had left in his room was still burning. Nothing had been displaced. But a sheet of letter-paper
lay on the table where it could not fail to be seen. On it these
words were written:

My fiancée went off, leaving word that she could not be my wife,
that she was a dressmaker, not a princess. I don't know which way
to turn. I'm going away. I have no wish to live. I hope Yvonne will
forgive me for not saying good-bye, but there is nothing she could
do for me . . .

The candle sputtered and went out. Meaulnes turned away,
closed the door, and went back into his own room. In spite of
the darkness he had no difficulty in finding the things he had
laid out a few hours since, when there was still daylight, when
he was still happy. One by one, like old friends, he recovered
each worn and shabby item of his wardrobe, from his clumsy
boots to his heavy belt with its brass buckle. He changed

quickly, but absent-mindedly, folding his borrowed garments over a chair, and leaving the wrong waistcoat behind.

Under the window, out in the carriage yard, there was a scene of utter confusion. Pulling, pushing, and yelling, each man was intent on disengaging his own vehicle from the jam. Now and then someone swinging a lantern would climb to the seat of a cart or the roof of a coach, and as the flare crossed the window the room, now so familiar to Meaulnes, peopled with objects which had been so friendly, seemed for a moment to breathe and come to life . . . And as he carefully closed the door behind him, this was the last impression he had of the mysterious lodging he might never set eyes on again.

17

THE STRANGE FÊTE

CONCLUSION

ALREADY a line of carriages was advancing slowly through the darkness towards the gate in the wood. At their head walked a man in a goat-skin jacket holding a dark-lantern and leading the first horse by the bridle.

Meaulnes was in haste to find someone to give him a lift, in haste to be off. He had now a deep-seated dread of being left alone in the domain and shown up for a fraud.

When he reached the main entrance he found the drivers of the rearmost wagons adjusting the balance of their loads: passengers were being asked to stand while seats were drawn back or forward. Girls swathed in fichus got up with difficulty; rugs slipped from their laps; and as they stooped to retrieve them their faces looked strained in the disk of light cast by the carriage-lamps.

In one of these drivers Meaulnes recognized the young peasant who had offered him a lift.

'May I get in?' he called out.

But he himself had not been recognized. 'Which way are you going, mate?'

'Sainte-Agathe.'

'Then you'd better try Maritain.'

He searched among the belated travellers for a man he didn't know. In the end Maritain was identified as one of the group still drinking and singing in the kitchen.

'He's a rare one for a good time,' someone remarked. 'He'll be there till three in the morning.'

Meaulnes's thoughts flew to the unhappy girl sick with anxiety, spending a feverish night while these louts filled her house with their singing. Where, he wondered, was her room? In what part of these mysterious precincts was her window to be seen? But no purpose could be served by delaying his departure. He must get away. Once back at Sainte-Agathe his impressions would sort themselves out; he would no longer be a schoolboy playing truant; he would be free to dream of the young lady of the château.

One by one the carriages moved away, their wheels grinding the sand of the long avenue. He saw them turn and disappear into the night laden with women in shawls and children swaddled in mufflers and already asleep. A large carriole set off; a wagonette in which women sat shoulder to shoulder – and Meaulnes was left standing in dismay on the threshold of the house. The only chance now was an old Berlin in charge of a peasant wearing a smock.

'Get in, then,' he said when Meaulnes had explained his plight. 'We're going your way.'

With difficulty Meaulnes opened the door of the ramshackle coach, making the window-pane rattle and the hinges creak. At one end of the seat two small children, a boy and a girl, were sleeping. The noise and the cold air woke them; they stretched, stared vaguely, shivered, and then huddled back into their corner and went to sleep again . . .

As the old carriage got into motion Meaulnes closed the door more gently and settled cautiously into the other corner of the seat. Then, avidly, he kept his eyes at the window trying to fix in memory the topography of the scene he was leaving behind and the route by which he had first come to it. In the dark he half saw, half guessed his surroundings as the carriage felt its way through garden and courtyard, past the stairway to his room, into the avenue, through the gateway, out to the road through the wood where the trunks of old fir trees went past the window in procession.

'We may overtake Frantz de Galais,' he thought, and his heart beat faster.

Abruptly the carriage swerved to avoid an obstacle in the narrow road. Out of the night something huge loomed up that looked like a house on wheels; it could only be a caravan which had been left standing there, within easy reach, during the festivities.

Once past this obstruction, the horses began to trot. Meaulnes was growing tired of peering through the window into a fog of darkness when suddenly, in the wood, there was a flash and a detonation. The horses broke into a gallop and at first Meaulnes was not sure whether the man on the box was trying to hold them in or urging them on. He tried to open the door, but it was stuck, and he shook it in vain . . . The children, awake now and frightened, pressed close to one another but made no sound. And while he was struggling with the door, his face close to the window-pane, the carriage-lamp flashing for an instant on a bend in the road revealed a white figure running, haggard and distraught. It was the pierrot of the fête, the strolling player still in costume, holding a body in his arms. Then everything was blotted out.

Inside the carriage, now hurtling through the night, the two children had again settled down to sleep. There was no one to whom Meaulnes could speak of the mysterious happenings of these last two days. For a long while he revolved in his mind all he had seen and heard until, weary and heavy-hearted, the young man too gave himself up to sleep, like a disconsolate child . . .

. . . It was not yet dawn when the carriage came to a stop and Meaulnes was roused by a tap on the window. With difficulty the driver opened the stubborn door, letting in the cold night wind which struck through to the bone.

'This is where you get out,' the driver was saying. 'I turn

off here. It will soon be light now, and you're not far from Sainte-Agathe.'

Cramped and numb, automatically obedient, Meaulnes felt around vaguely for his cap which had fallen at the feet of the sleeping children in the darkest corner of the coach, then bent down and stepped out into the road.

The man in the smock said good-bye and climbed back to his seat. 'You've only six kilometres to walk,' he said. 'There's a milestone over there on the side of the road.'

Still drugged with sleep, Meaulnes walked with heavy feet and stooped shoulders towards the landmark and sat down. He crossed his arms and let his head fall drowsily forward . . .

But the driver expostulated. 'You mustn't go to sleep there! You'll freeze! . . . Up you get now . . . You'll soon walk it off . . .'

Staggering like a drunkard, hands in his pockets, shoulders hunched, he trudged along the road to Sainte-Agathe while the old Berlin – last vestige of a mysterious fête – wheeled away from the gravelled road and went lurching noiselessly across country over a grass-grown track. Beyond the hedge nothing could be seen of it but the driver's cap bobbing up and down . . .

PART TWO

I

PIRATES

THE cold weather – the high winds, the snow, and the rain – the impossibility of doing any useful exploring as long as winter lasted, discouraged further talk between Meaulnes and me about the lost domain. Nothing worth while could be attempted during the short days of February, not even on the Thursdays, our weekly holiday, which began with a series of squalls that invariably turned into a steady sleet by five o'clock.

There was nothing to remind us of his adventure but the fact – and it seemed very odd – that since the afternoon of his return we had had no friends. During breaks, the same games were played as before, but Jasmin was no longer on speaking terms with *le grand Meaulnes*. When school was finished for the day and the rooms swept out, the yard emptied as quickly as in the days when I was alone, and I watched my companion wander from the garden to the playground shelter, from the yard to the dining-room.

On Thursday mornings we sat in one of the two class-rooms reading books by Rousseau and Paul-Louis Courier which we had found in a cupboard among English Methods and note-books filled with neatly copied musical scores. Again, in the afternoon, if we wanted to get away from women visitors, we fled from the house to the class-rooms . . . Sometimes we heard a group of the older boys who would pause in front of the big gateway as if by chance, then lunge at it as though performing some incomprehensible military manoeuvre, and finally go away . . . Things went on in this gloomy sort of way till late in February. I was beginning to think Meaulnes had forgotten, when a fresh adventure, stranger than all the rest, showed not only how wrong I was, but how blind to the forces which, beneath all this winter stagnation, were working up to a crisis.

It was in fact on a Thursday night towards the end of the month that the first news of the strange domain, the first small wave from the adventure we no longer spoke of, reached our shore. We had settled down for the evening. My grandparents having gone home, only Millie and my father were with us, and they had no inkling of the secret feud that divided the class into two clans.

At eight o'clock Millie opened the door to throw out some crumbs she had swept from the table, and her voice, as she exclaimed, 'Ah!' was so clear that we went to see for ourselves. The doorstep was carpeted with snow. As it was too dark to see anything I stepped out into the yard to ascertain how deep the snow was. I felt light flakes on my cheek which melted at once. Then Millie, shivering, called me in and shut the door.

At nine we were about to go up to bed – my mother had already picked up the lamp – when we distinctly heard two heavy blows on the big gate at the entrance to the courtyard. Millie put down the lamp and we stood there straining our ears.

To find out what was happening meant going out into the snow with the lamp, which would only be extinguished and probably broken before we had got half-way across the yard. For a moment there was no further sound and my father was saying, 'I dare say it's only . . .' when, right under the dining-room window which, as I have said, gave on the station road, a whistle blew – a shrill, prolonged note that could have been heard as far away as the church. It was immediately followed by shouts outside the window where invaders must have hoisted themselves up on the outer wall supports. They were screaming:

'Hand him over! Hand him over!'

The cry was taken up by a group at the other extremity of the premises who must have approached through old Martin's field and got over the wall separating it from our playground.

Then from every direction unfamiliar or disguised voices, eight or ten of them one after another, kept howling: 'Hand him over!' They came from the roof of the storehouse which could be reached over a pile of firewood stacked against the outer wall; from the low wall between the shelter and the gateway whose rounded top was convenient for straddling; from the wall bordering the station road which could be scaled by means of the iron gate . . . And to complete the circle, belated reinforcements, having got into the garden, added a piratical variation to the theme by yelling:

'Board them! Board them!'

By now the uproar was echoing through the vacant classrooms where windows had been forced.

Meaulnes and I were so familiar with each twist and turn and vantage-point in the rambling structures that we could follow as if on a map every move of the unknown raiders.

For that matter it was only in the first moment of surprise that we felt any alarm. At the sound of the whistle all four of us had jumped to the same conclusion: that we were in for an attack by a band of marauders. As it happened a ruffianly sort of man accompanied by a young fellow with a bandaged head had stationed his caravan in the Square behind the church, and they had been hanging about the village for at least a fortnight. Other doubtful characters had also come into the neighbourhood recently looking for work among the smiths and wheelwrights.

But when we heard the shouting we knew we had local men, or more likely mere youths, to deal with. In fact, to judge from some of the high-pitched voices, there were young boys among the pirates swarming the sides of our house as if it were a ship at sea.

'Well, I'll be . . .' my father began, and Millie broke in:

'What on earth can it be?'

Suddenly, at the gates, on the wall, then outside the window, the shouting broke off. And just beyond the window-sash we heard two more blasts of the whistle. The cries from the roof of the storehouse and from the garden began to die down and finally ceased. And now we could hear the muffled sound of troops in flight past the dining-room wall, their thudding boots cushioned by the snow.

Obviously someone had disturbed them. At a time of night when honest folk are in their beds they had counted on being unmolested in their raid on an isolated house at the edge of the village. But something had gone wrong . . .

We had barely had time to collect ourselves – for their approach had been as stealthy as that of a well-led boarding party – when, just as we were about to investigate, we heard a neighbourly voice calling out from the street:

'Monsieur Seurel! Monsieur Seurel!'

It was Monsieur Pasquier, the butcher. Before coming in, the fat little man scraped his sabots and shook the snow from his smock. Then with the cunning air of one who, not without peril, has laid bare a conspiracy, he began:

'I happened to be out in my yard which faces the Four-Roads. I was just going to shut the stable where I keep my goats. All of a sudden, what do I see out there in the snow? Two tall fellows standing there like sentinels, or on the look-out for something. They were just by the Cross. I move closer. I haven't taken more than two steps when – hp! they're off at the double down your way. So I lost no time. I got my lantern and I said to myself: "I'll just nip down and tell Monsieur Seurel" . . .'

A pause for breath, and then taking up his story where it began:

'There I was, out in the yard behind the house . . .'

We interrupt him by the offer of a liqueur, which he accepts, and we ply him with questions, asking for details which he is unable to supply.

He had seen nothing out of the ordinary on his way to our house. The troops, alerted by the two watchers he had surprised, had simply melted away. As to the identity of this pair, he could only make a guess:

'Might have been those two mountebanks. For a month or so they've been hanging about in the Square, waiting for the weather to break so they can put on their show . . . No telling what they've been up to . . .'

This got us no farther and we stood in perplexity while Monsieur Pasquier sipped his liqueur and resumed his story with more gestures than facts, when Meaulnes, who up to then had been listening intently, picked up the butcher's lantern and made for the door.

'We'll soon find out,' he said.

We followed him: Monsieur Seurel, Monsieur Pasquier, and I.

Millie, reassured by the departure of the marauders, and like all fastidious, methodical persons, somewhat lacking in curiosity, called out as we left:

'Well, go if you want to. But be sure to close the door and take the key. I'm going to bed. I'll leave the lamp burning.'

2

THE AMBUSH

IN dead silence we set off through the snow. Meaulnes walked ahead, preceded by a fan of light cast by the dark-lantern . . . But we had scarcely got through the big gateway when from behind the municipal weighing-scales which flanked the wall of our playground two hooded figures scuttled off like startled partridges. Whether as a challenge, or whether they were merely carried away by the exhilaration of their strange game and the nervous fear of being caught, they flung a few mocking words back at us as they took to their heels.

Meaulnes dropped the lantern on the snow and said:

'Follow me, François!'

Leaving behind the two older and less agile men we sprinted off in pursuit of the two shadows who, after a short detour round the lower end of the village along the lane from the Vieille-Planche, swung back deliberately in the direction of the church. They ran stealthily, not too fast, and we had no trouble in keeping them in sight. They crossed the church road where everything was wrapped in sleep, then made for a maze of little streets and blind alleys beyond the graveyard.

This quarter, known as the 'odd corners', was inhabited

mostly by day-labourers, weavers, and dressmakers. We were not well acquainted with it and had never been there at night. By day it was deserted enough – the workmen away on their jobs, the weavers cooped up indoors – by night even more so; and in the deep silence it seemed even sounder asleep than the rest of the village. Which made it all the less likely that anyone would show up at a pinch to lend us a hand.

I was familiar with only one of these narrow streets that wound their way between small box-like houses that seemed to have been set down there by accident, and that was the one that led to the house of a dressmaker we knew as the dumb woman. You went first down a fairly steep slope paved here and there with flagstones, then, after two or three twists, past empty stables and weavers' yards, till you came to a wide impasse blocked by a farm long since abandoned. On visits to the dumb woman, while she carried on a silent conversation with my mother, her fingers wriggling, her muteness lapsing occasionally into weak little cries, I had sat at her window looking down over the high wall of this farm, beyond which the open country began. The entrance to the farmyard was barred by a gate that remained closed. In the yard itself there was not so much as a bale of straw, still less any sign of animation...

It was along this very route that the chase was leading us. At every turning we were afraid the quarry would give us the slip, but to my surprise, whenever they turned into a side-street, we came in sight of them before they had swung into the next one. I say 'to my surprise' because these narrow passages were so short that they could have eluded us quite easily if they had really tried to.

At last they ran straight into the street on which our dress-maker lived, and I shouted to Meaulnes:

'We've got them cornered – it's a blind alley.'

But it was they who had cornered us, having deliberately led us to a spot well suited to their purpose. On reaching the wall they turned to face us, and one of them gave the whistling signal we had heard twice before that evening.

Immediately a band of young fellows, perhaps ten in num-

ber, emerged from the deserted farmyard where they must
have been lying in wait. They had wound mufflers around their
faces and pulled up the hoods of their capes . . .

A needless precaution, because we already knew who they
were. Besides, we hadn't the faintest intention of carrying tales
to Monsieur Seurel; this concerned us alone. Delouche, Denis,
Giraudat were there – the whole clan in fact. We recognized
them by their way of fighting and by their grunts and splutters.
But there was one disturbing factor in the situation – even
Meaulnes seemed alarmed by it. One of the group was unknown to us, and it was he who seemed to be the ringleader . . .

He didn't touch Meaulnes himself; he kept an eye on his
soldiers, who for that matter were having a rough time, being
dragged over the snow, their clothing in shreds, as they con-
centrated their attack on my tall but hard-pressed companion.
Two of them had singled me out, and though I fought with all
my might, they at last got me down on my heels where I was
forced to remain, knees bended, my wrists held behind my
back, so that I could do nothing but watch the battle with a
mixture of fright and intense curiosity.

Meaulnes was in the grip of four of his classmates who
clung to his smock. But by a sudden sharp twist he caught
them off balance and swung them into the snow . . . Meanwhile
the unknown personage, standing aloof, followed each move
with a cool intensity, issuing orders in a clear voice:

'That's it! . . . Don't be afraid . . . Follow it up . . .' and then
the English words: 'Go on, my boys! . . .'

It was obvious that he was the one in full command . . .
Where had he come from? Where had he trained them for
battle, and by what means? We had no clue to the mystery.
Like the others he had wound a muffler about his face, but
when Meaulnes, having shaken himself free for the moment,
advanced on him, the movement he made to put himself on
guard revealed the edge of something white that looked as if it
might be a bandage round his head . . .

It was at this moment that I gave a sudden shout:

'Meaulnes! Look out! There's another one behind you!'

His back was against the fence barring the entrance to the

farmyard, and before he could wheel round a great long-legged fellow who had been concealed in the yard slipped a scarf round his neck, yanking his head backwards. In a flash the four assailants who had been flung down in the snow came back to the charge and pinned down his arms and legs. Then they bound his wrists with cord and his ankles with someone's muffler . . . The youth with the bandaged head began to go through my friend's pockets, while the second stranger, the man with the lasso, lit a candle-end, shielding the flame with his hand. By its light the young ringleader examined every scrap of paper he found, and at last he unfolded the rough sketch covered with notes on which Meaulnes had been working ever since his return.

'This is it!' he cried exultantly. 'Here's our map! Here's our guide-book! We'll soon see whether this gentleman went where I think he did . . .'

His confederates blew out the candle. His troops picked up their caps and belts and dispersed as silently as they had arrived. And I was left alone to untie my companion, which I did as quickly as I could.

'With that map he won't get very far,' said Meaulnes as he got to his feet.

We turned homewards, walking slowly, for he was limping.

In the church road we met Monsieur Seurel and Monsieur Pasquier.

'You didn't see anything?' said my father. 'Nor did we.'

Luckily it was too dark for them to notice our dishevelled state.

So the butcher took his leave, and Monsieur Seurel lost no time in getting to bed.

But we two, up in our room, by the light of the lamp Millie had left us, were patching our torn smocks till well into the night while in lowered voices we reviewed all that had happened, like comrades-in-arms after a day of reverses . . .

3

THE VAGABOND AT SCHOOL

GETTING up next morning was a painful business. At half past eight, just as Monsieur Seurel was giving the signal to go into class, we arrived out of breath, and being late were prepared to squeeze in wherever we could find a place. Usually *le grand Meaulnes* was at the head of the line, the first to pass inspection as we waited elbow to elbow armed with texts, notebooks, and pens.

I was surprised at the alacrity everyone showed as if on some tacit understanding, to make room for us in the middle of the line, and while the master, holding up our entrance for a few moments, was inspecting Meaulnes, I ventured to peer into the faces of our overnight foes standing to right and left of me.

The first enemy to catch my eye was the very one I had been thinking about for hours, and certainly the last person I expected to see in these surroundings. Moreover, he was in the place always occupied by Meaulnes at the head of the line, one foot resting on the stone step as he leaned against the doorpost with a knapsack cushioning his shoulder. His face was finely featured, very pale, slightly freckled, and he was looking us over with an expression of mingled curiosity, amusement, and condescension. His head and one side of his face were swathed in white dressings. I recognized the leader of the gang, the young vagrant who had robbed us the night before.

But roll-call was over and we went to our places. The new pupil sat near the stanchion that supported the ceiling, on the left side of the bench whose extreme right was occupied by Meaulnes. Giraudat, Delouche, and the three other occupants of this first row had crowded together to make room for him, as if it had all been planned in advance . . .

Often during the winter we had these stray pupils: young men from the barges caught in the ice of the canal, apprentices, snowbound travellers. They would stay in class for a few days, a month, seldom longer. Objects of curiosity for a while, they soon found their level and ceased to attract attention.

But this one was not so soon to be forgotten. I can still see that odd creature and all the strange treasures he had brought in his knapsack. First there were the 'picture' penholders he produced when it was time to take down dictation: if you closed one eye you could see, through an eyelet in the handle, an enlarged if somewhat blurred view of the Basilica of Lourdes or some less familiar monument. He chose one for himself and the others passed from hand to hand. Next came a Chinese pencil-box containing a pair of compasses and other curious instruments. This too passed down the line, slipping silently from hand to hand under the exercise-books so that Monsieur Seurel would not see.

Then a collection of clean new books whose titles I knew from greedy examination of rare volumes in our library: a book about blackbirds, another about sea-gulls, one called 'My friend Benoist' . . . These books, wherever they came from, and perhaps they'd been stolen, were being examined by boys who held them on their knee with one hand, taking down dictation with the other. One lad described circles with the compass inside his desk. Others, the moment the master's back was turned as he paced to and fro while dictating, would close one eye and glue the other on a glaucous and spotty view of Notre Dame de Paris. From time to time the new pupil, pen in hand, his delicate profile outlined against the grey post, would wink connivingly at these furtive goings-on.

But uneasiness was gradually spreading through the room, for all these objects, systematically relayed, had been arriving one after the other in the hands of *le grand Meaulnes* who put them down without even bothering to look at them. Before long there was a heap on his desk, a pattern of shapes and colours as diversified as the miscellany you see at the feet of the woman called 'Science' in allegorical frescoes. Even Monsieur Seurel could not fail to notice such a conspicuous display and discover what was going on. Besides, he must have been contemplating an inquiry into the events of the previous night. The vagabond's presence would facilitate his task . . .

And indeed it was not long before he was brought up short in front of Meaulnes's desk.

Waving his book at the bizarre exhibition, his index finger holding the place between the pages, he demanded: 'Who does all that belong to?'

'I've no idea,' muttered Meaulnes without lifting his head.

The new-comer spoke up at once:

'They're mine.'

But with a courtly gesture which quite disarmed the old man, he quickly added: 'They're entirely at your disposition, Monsieur, if you'd care to examine them.'

Within a few seconds, but quietly, so as not to endanger the welcome new mood, the whole class had crept up and clustered around the master, whose curly head with its bald spot was bent over these curiosities, while the pallid young stranger calmly and with great complacency explained their uses and merits.

Le grand Meaulnes had not moved from his place. In complete isolation, his waste-book open before him, a frown on his forehead, he was wrestling with a difficult problem.

We were still engrossed in all this when it was time for the morning break. Dictation had been left in the air and all pretence of work abandoned. Indeed the whole morning so far had been a recreation period. Moreover, at half past ten when we were let loose into the dull and muddy yard, it was obvious that we had acquired a new games master.

Of all the many diversions we owed to the vagabond student from that time on, the only one I clearly remember was the most ruthless: a sort of tournament in which the knights were the younger boys mounted on the shoulders of the biggest. Divided into two teams and lined up on opposite sides of the yard, they charged at a signal, each trying to dismount his adversary by the violence of the shock. For want of weapons the knights used their mufflers as lassos, their arms as lances. Some, in side-stepping the onslaught, lost their balance and went sprawling in the mud, horse over rider. Other knights, sliding down the neck of their chargers, were

dragged back to the saddle by their own horses and headed
into the fray. Mounted on Delage – a young giant with red
hair and donkey's ears – the slim knight of the bandaged head
laughingly egged on the rival teams, handling his own steed
with great cunning.

Augustin, still out of sorts, stood in the doorway looking
on, his hands in his pockets. I stood near him, hesitant.

'He's pretty sly,' he muttered. 'Turning up here the very
next morning! The one way to divert suspicion from himself.
And Monsieur Seurel rose to it.'

His cropped head bare to the wind, he stood for some time
fuming against this mountebank now directing the slaughter of
the very troops who had so recently rallied round him. And
being a peaceable sort of boy I could only agree.

Even in odd corners of the yard or on the margin of the
battlefield itself the smaller boys, mounted one upon the
other, staggered about and tumbled down even before being
attacked . . . Soon the only horses still valid formed a whirling,
milling group in the centre of the yard, where above the mêlée
one caught glimpses of the leader's white bandage.

At last *le grand Meaulnes* could no longer resist. Bending
down, his hands on his thighs, he turned to me:

'Come on, François!'

Taken by surprise, but with alacrity, I climbed on his
shoulders and we lunged into action. Whereupon most of the
remaining combatants made off in a panic crying out:

'Look out, chaps, here's Meaulnes . . . *Le grand Meaulnes!*'

Advancing on those left behind, Meaulnes began to whirl
round, exhorting me:

'Stretch out your arm and grab them the way I did last
night.'

My blood was up, and certain of victory I reached out right
and left, seizing my opponents, making them totter, pushing
them off their mounts into the mud. In no time we had
accounted for all but the new-comer astride Delage. But
Delage was none too eager to pit himself against an adversary
of Augustin's mettle and suddenly arching his back brought
the pale knight to his feet. He stood for a moment, his hand on

Delage's shoulder, like a young captain holding the check-rein of his charger, and gazed at *le grand Meaulnes* as if surprised into open admiration.

'Well done!' he said.

But just then the bell rang, dispersing the group which had gathered round us in the hope of exciting developments. And Augustin, cross and surly at having been denied the satisfaction of unhorsing his enemy, turned away muttering:

'It's only postponed.'

Until noon lessons proceeded in a pre-holiday atmosphere, relieved by amusing interludes and talk, all centring on the actor-student.

He said they were camping in the Square till the cold spell was over, for there was no point in putting on shows that nobody would come to. To fill in the time they had decided that he should go back to school while his partner looked after the tropical birds and the trained goat. He told us about their roving life in the neighbouring countryside, how the rain pelted down on the sleazy zinc roof of their caravan, how it got stuck on the country lanes and how they would have to get out and push. Boys in the back rows edged forward to listen, the more practical ones taking the opportunity to get warm by the stove, though even they were soon curious enough to crane forward to listen, keeping one hand on the fire-guard to make sure of not losing their place.

'And what do you live on?' asked Monsieur Seurel who had a schoolmaster's somewhat naïve curiosity and was asking more and more questions.

The young man looked blank. Apparently he hadn't given the matter much thought.

'Why, on our takings during the autumn, I suppose. I leave all that to Ganache.'

Who Ganache might be, no one bothered to inquire. But in my mind's eye I saw the lanky ruffian who had stolen up on Meaulnes from behind and so treacherously put him out of action . . .

4

A LINK WITH THE MYSTERIOUS DOMAIN

THE afternoon session provided still further diversions, and study was scamped again in favour of much underhand activity. The vagabond had brought a fresh stock: shells, games, songs – even a little monkey which kept scratching at the lining of the knapsack . . . Every few moments Monsieur Seurel would break off in the middle of a lesson to see what new prodigy this rogue had conjured up . . . When four o'clock struck, the only pupil who had done his problems was Meaulnes.

No one was in a hurry to leave. There was no longer, it seemed, the sharp line of demarcation between work and recreation that had made our ordinary school life as simple and regular as the succession of night and day. For one thing we had forgotten the daily rite of designating the monitors. This was a most unusual lapse. Normally, at ten minutes to four, we would tell Monsieur Seurel the names of two pupils who would stay and sweep up. And we never failed to do this, as it had a way of winding things up for the day.

As it happened, Augustin was down on the rota, and during the morning I had explained to our vagabond that he would be paired with Meaulnes, as every new pupil was expected to help with the sweeping on his first day in class.

Meaulnes went off for a moment to get some bread for his afternoon snack but when he came back to the school-room there was no sign of our visitor. When he did turn up, out of breath from running, it was already getting dark . . .

I had stayed behind at Augustin's request. 'While I hold him,' he had said, 'you take the map from him.'

So I sat at a desk near the window, reading by the last rays of daylight, while they went about their task, moving the benches about without saying a word – *le grand Meaulnes* looking grim in his black smock with its three buttons at the back, his belt drawn tight; the other slight, nervous, with a bandaged head. He had on a shabby overcoat with rents in it I hadn't noticed before. He was putting a kind of fierce ardour into his efforts, lifting and pushing the desks with feverish haste, a half smile on his lips. He might have been playing some strange game whose object was known only to himself.

They had reached the darkest corner of the big room and were moving the last of the desks.

In that corner, with a turn of the wrist, Meaulnes could have floored his adversary without being seen from a window or even heard outside. I wondered why he should let such an opportunity go by. In a moment the enemy would be moving towards the door; he would slip out on the pretext that the job was done and we should never see him again. The map, and all the bits of information Meaulnes had taken so long to collect and verify and note down, would be lost for good . . .

At any moment I was expecting my comrade to make me some sign that the battle was joined; but his attitude never changed. Except that every now and then he would stare rather oddly, questioningly, at the bandage on which, even in the growing twilight, I could now see a wide dark stain.

The last desk was replaced, and still no sign.

But when they were walking back with their brooms to tidy the last patch near the door Meaulnes, without looking up at our enemy, said in a chastened sort of voice:

'There's blood on your bandage; and your clothes are torn.'

The young man looked at him a moment, not in surprise at the remark itself, but deeply touched that he should make it.

'They tried to get your map away from me,' he said. 'A little while ago. In the Square. When they heard I was coming back to help sweep they guessed I was going to make peace with you, and they revolted. But I saved it in spite of them,' he added proudly, and handed Meaulnes the precious sheet of folded paper.

Meaulnes turned round slowly. 'You hear that, François? There he was, fighting for us and getting wounded, while we set a trap for him.'

93

Then, for the first time addressing him as an equal, he held out his hand and said:

'You're a real friend.'

The strolling player took his hand, and for a moment remained speechless, too deeply stirred to find voice. But his intense curiosity soon set his tongue in motion again:

'So you were setting a trap for me! The funny part of it is, I suspected as much, and I said to myself: "What a surprise they'll get when they look at their map and see I've filled it in" . . .'

'Filled it in!'

'Well, not completely . . . You see . . .'

Abruptly his sprightliness disappeared. He drew closer to us and his voice grew solemn as he went on, speaking deliberately:

'It's time I told you, Meaulnes: I went there too, where you were. I was at that extraordinary fête. And when the boys here spoke of some strange adventure you'd had, I felt sure it had some connexion with that old lost domain. To make certain, I had to get hold of your map . . . But, like you, I don't know the name of the château; I wouldn't know how to get back to it. Nor do I know the whole of the route that would take you there from here.'

With what eagerness, what burning curiosity, with what feelings of friendship we hemmed him in! Meaulnes questioned him greedily. It seemed to us that if we pressed our new friend hard enough we should learn from him the very thing he professed not to know.

'You'll see, you'll see,' the youth kept saying, as if annoyed, and slightly embarrassed. 'I've added a few landmarks that were missing on your map . . . That's all I could do.'

Then, noticing our enthusiasm and admiration:

'I'd better warn you,' he said, and there was pride in his tone despite its despondency, 'I'm not like other chaps. Three months ago I tried to put a bullet in my brain. That accounts for the bandage. Like one of those civilians called up in 1870 . . .'

'And tonight,' said Meaulnes gently, 'the wound opened again while you were fighting.'

94

But this time he was not to be moved, and went on with a hint of bravado:

'I wanted to die. But as I bungled it, I'm only going to live for what fun I can get out of it, like a child, like a vagabond. I've turned my back on everything: I've no father, no sister, no home, no one to love . . . I've got nothing now, except chance play-fellows.'

'And they've let you down already,' I remarked.

'Yes, they have,' he said sharply. 'That fellow Delouche is at the bottom of it. He guessed I was going to make it up with you chaps. So he demoralized my troops, just when I had them so well in hand. You saw for yourself last night – that boarding party! Wasn't that a smart performance? Not since I was a child have I organized anything quite so successful . . .'

He remained pensive a moment, and then as if to dispel any final illusions on our part:

'If I've come over to you two tonight, it's only because – and it was this morning I became aware of it – there's more fun to be had with you than with all that gang. Especially that silly ass Delouche – trying to play the man at seventeen! The sort of thing I simply can't stand . . . Any chance of evening the score with him?'

'Nothing easier,' said Meaulnes. 'But will you be staying here long?'

'I don't know. I would like very much to stay. I'm terribly alone. I've no one but Ganache . . .'

Again all his sprightliness, his febrile vivacity, had fallen away. And he seemed for a moment to have sunk into the despair which must have overtaken him the day when the idea of suicide first entered his mind.

'Be my friends,' he suddenly said. 'Look here, I know your secret, and I've protected it from all of them. I can put you on the trail you've lost . . .'

Then with a kind of solemnity:

'Be my friends against the day when I shall be on the brink of hell, as I was once before . . . Swear you'll answer when I call – when I call like this . . .' (and he let out a strange sort of cry: Hou-ou) . . . 'You, Meaulnes, you swear first.'

And we took our oath, for, children that we were, anything a little more solemn and more serious than life enchanted us.

'And in return, here's one thing I *can* tell you: the address in Paris where the young lady of the château used to spend the holidays: Easter, Whitsun, the month of June, and sometimes part of the winter . . .'

At that moment a voice, unknown to us, came out of the night from the direction of the gateway: a call several times repeated. We guessed it to be Ganache the mountebank, who either didn't dare or didn't know how to cross the courtyard. The voice sounded urgent and anxious, as it cried out now loudly, now more softly:

'Hou-ou . . . Hou-ou . . .'

'Quickly! Tell me quickly,' Meaulnes begged the young vagrant, who had shuddered and was already buttoning up his overcoat to go.

Hastily he mentioned a Paris address which we repeated under our breath. Then he ran off through the shadows to join the companion waiting at the gate, leaving our minds in a turmoil impossible to describe.

5

A MAN WEARING *ESPADRILLES*

THAT night, or rather next morning, for it happened around three o'clock, Jasmin's mother, whose inn was situated in the centre of the village, got up to light her fire. Her brother-in-law, Dumas, who lived at the inn, had to set out on the road at four, and the rather pathetic creature, whose right hand had once been badly burned and was twisted out of shape, hurried down to the gloomy kitchen to make coffee. It was cold. She put on an old shawl over her night-clothes after turning up the corners of her apron to make a receptacle for kindling. Then, holding a candle in one hand and sheltering it with the other – the damaged one – she hurried out into a yard obstructed with crates and empty bottles and made her way to a shed where

firewood was kept. This shed also served as a hen-coop . . .
But no sooner had she got the door open than something went
swishing through the air: a long arm brandishing a cap. It
put out the candle and knocked her over, and as she went
down she was aware of someone looming out of the darkness
and padding away to a frenzied accompaniment of cluckings
and crowings.

The intruder had carried off in a sack – as the poor widow
discovered as soon as she was on her feet – a dozen of her
finest birds.

Her screams brought her brother-in-law running. To him it
was soon clear that the thief had got into the yard with a skele-
ton key and gone out the same way, for the door had been left
ajar. And as a man used to the ways of poachers and marauders
he immediately lit a carriage-lamp, and with this in one hand, a
loaded gun in the other, he set out to follow the tracks of the
thief. They were blurred, from which he concluded that his
man was wearing canvas shoes with rope soles – *espadrilles*.
But he was able to follow the trail along the station road as far
as a fence which closed off a meadow, and here it came to an
end. Obliged to give up this clue he looked up, stood still –
and heard in the distance, but on the same road, a vehicle of
some sort being driven away at a gallop: in short, making its
escape . . .

Meanwhile Jasmin had got up, reached for his cape, and run
out in his slippers to inspect the neighbourhood. The sleeping
village was plunged in the stillness that precedes the first light
of day. On reaching the Four-Roads he heard, like his uncle,
far off on the Riaudes hillside, the sound of wheels and pounding hoofs. Being a sly sort of fellow who couldn't help boast-
ing even when alone, he said to himself then, and next day to
us, rolling his *r*'s in the detestable accent of the suburbs of
Montluçon:

'That lot got away down the station road, but it wouldn't
surprise me if I started a hare on the other side of the village.'

And in the deep silence of the night he turned and headed
towards the church.

When he got to the Square he saw that there was a light in

97

the caravan, as if someone were ill. He was going over to make
inquiries when, from the direction of the 'odd corners' a
human shadow, shod with *espadrilles* came running, swift and
silent, without looking to right or left, and stopped, panting,
at the steps of the caravan.

Having identified the shadow as Ganache, Jasmin suddenly
stepped forward into the little circle of light and whispered:

'What's up? Anything wrong?'

Haggard, dishevelled, toothless, Ganache stared at him in
fright for a moment before gasping out:

'It's my mate. He's bad . . . He got into a fight last night and
it started his head bleeding again. I've been to fetch the
nurse . . .'

And in fact as Jasmin Delouche was walking homewards,
consumed with curiosity, he did meet a Sister of Mercy hurrying along the main street of the village.

When day broke, several inhabitants of Sainte-Agathe
appeared at their front door with the dull and puffy eyes of
people who have spent a sleepless night. From each of them
issued cries of outrage and indignation which spread through
the village like a train of gunpowder.

At the Giraudat's, around two o'clock, two women who
were alone in the house were wakened by a carriole which
stood under their windows and into which someone was hastily
dumping bundles that fell with a soft impact. They were too
frightened to stir. But in the morning a brief inspection of their
back-yard established the fact that those bundles were rabbits
and poultry . . . Millie, during the morning break, found
several half-burnt matches outside the wash-house door and
deduced that the marauders had been misinformed about our
premises and were unable to find a way in . . . At Perreux's, at
Boujardon's, and at Clément's pigs were missing as well, but
later in the morning all the quadrupeds were rounded up in
various gardens where they were tranquilly rooting for let-
tuces, having been tempted by the open doors to indulge in a
nocturnal promenade . . . Nearly everywhere fowls had been
stolen, but nothing else. Madame Pignot, who kept a bake-

shop but no chickens, complained loud and long that she had been robbed of a washing beetle and a pound of blue, but this theft was never proved, nor inscribed on the official report . . .

This breeze of frenzy and fear and chatter kept blowing all morning. In class Jasmin related his night's adventure:

'They're wily all right,' he concluded. 'But if my uncle had run into one of them, as he himself said, he'd have shot him down like a rabbit.'

Then, with a glance in our direction:

'Lucky he didn't run into Ganache; he'd have thought nothing of potting him one. They're all alike, that rabble,' he said. And Dessaigne said the same.

Our new friends, however, were left in peace. It was only on the following evening that Jasmin pointed out to his uncle that Ganache, like the thief, went about in *espadrilles*. They agreed that this coincidence was worth bringing to the attention of the police. So it was decided that, as soon as they could find time, they would make a secret visit to the principal town of the canton and give a hint to the head of the police in person.

During the days that followed there was no sign of the young man whose head wound had reopened.

In the evenings we roamed about the church square, if only to catch a glimpse of the lamp showing behind the red curtain of the caravan. Anxious and restless, we hovered there without daring to go near the humble little house on wheels that, for us, represented a mysterious entrance to the domain towards which we could find no other approach.

6

A DISPUTE BEHIND THE SCENES

WITH so many disturbances and so much to worry about we had scarcely noticed that March was upon us and a new softness had come into the air. But on the third morning after these events, as I went down into the yard, I suddenly realized it was spring. A pleasant breeze, smooth as warm water, flowed over the wall. During the night a fine rain had washed the peony leaves; recently dug beds in the garden gave off an earthy smell you could almost taste; and in the branches of a tree near the window a bird was trying to learn music . . .

During the morning break Meaulnes suggested it was time to try out the route indicated by the vagabond-student's additions to our map. It was all I could do to persuade him to wait till we had seen our friend again, or at least till the weather was more settled, till the plum trees of Sainte-Agathe were in blossom. Leaning against the low wall, bare-headed, our hands in our pockets, we talked it over while the wind set us shivering one minute, only to disarm us in the next breath with a warm caress that stirred into life enthusiasms that had been lying dormant. Ah, brother, comrade, rover! How sure we were that felicity was within reach, that to attain it we had only to set our feet on the path . . .

Half-way through lunch we heard the roll of a drum and ran out, serviettes in hand, and stood on the step outside the little gate. It was Ganache, at the Four-Roads, announcing that 'thanks to the fine weather' there would be a full performance that evening at eight o'clock, in the open space in front of the church. But to provide against 'all contingencies' a tent would be erected. Then he read out a long list of attractions, but the wind carried off most of his words, though we caught a few of them: 'pantomimes . . . songs . . . equestrian fantasies . . .' each item punctuated by a roll of the drum.

During our evening meal this same big drum passed under the window, fairly rattling the panes, as a reminder that the show was about to begin. And soon people from the outskirts came straggling into the village; we could hear a buzz of conversation as they passed by in little groups on their way towards the church. And there we were, we two, obliged to sit through dinner, chafing with impatience.

At last, around nine, we heard a scraping of boots and stifled laughter at the small gate: the schoolmistresses had come to collect us. And we all set off in the dark towards the site where the show was to be given. From a distance we saw the walls of the church lit up as if by a bonfire. The wavering light came from two pressure lamps marking the entrance to the tent . . .

Inside, benches rose in tiers, circus fashion. Monsieur Seurel, the schoolmistresses, Meaulnes, and I found seats in the bottom row. Although it must have been a very small enclosure, in memory it is as big as a real circus, with vast dim areas packed with spectators among whom I see Madame Pignot, the baker-woman; Fernande who kept the grocery; girls of the village; men who worked in the smithies; wives of leading citizens; children; country folk – a throng . . .

The performance was more than half over. A little nanny-goat was performing in the arena, obediently placing her feet first on four glasses, then on two, finally on one. It was Ganache who put her through her paces, coaxing her with taps of a wand. He kept looking uneasily in our direction, his eyes lifeless, his mouth slack.

On a stool near two other lamps which were placed on either side of the curtain cutting off the arena from the caravan, the ring-master was seated. It was our friend. He wore elegant black tights and his head was bandaged.

We had just got settled when a pony in gay trappings cantered into the arena and circled two or three times under the guidance of the wounded youth. When ordered to indicate the most amiable or the most courageous member of the audience, the pony never failed to stop before one of our group. But he singled out Madame Pignot whenever he was asked to point out the most mendacious, the most miserly, or the most amorously inclined spectator present. This provoked much hilarity in her entourage and set up a chorus of cries and a cackling as of geese being harried by a spaniel . . .

During the interval the ring-master came over for a moment to chat with Monsieur Seurel, who could not have been more flattered if he had been addressed by Talma or Léotard. As for us, we drank in every word as he spoke of his wound – now closed – of the show they had been rehearsing during the long winter months – of their sojourn, which would be extended till the end of the month as they had several attractions in reserve for additional performances.

The spectacle was to end with a dumb show.

Towards the end of the interval our friend left us. To reach the caravan he had to cross the arena, where groups were now standing about, among them Jasmin Delouche, who had suddenly come in with the air of someone just back from a trip. The women and girls made way for the slight figure in black: his costume, his injury, something oddly courageous in his bearing had charmed every one of them. Meanwhile Jasmin was engaged in lively conversation with Madame Pignot, addressing her in low tones, though one felt that a sailor's red pompom, blue collar, and bell-bottomed trousers would have been more to her taste. Jasmin's thumbs were thrust under the lapels of his jacket and he stood there looking extremely conceited but also extremely put out. As the ring-master made his way through the group, Jasmin made some spiteful remark to Madame Pignot which I could not catch but which was loud enough to be heard by our friend and was certainly meant to be taken as an insult, or a provocation, or a threat. It must have been not only serious but unexpected, for the young man turned and stared, while Jasmin assumed an air of bravado, grinning, and nudging his neighbours as if to assure himself of support . . . All this took place in a matter of seconds, and I was probably the only person on our bench to notice it.

The ring-master turned away and went behind the curtain which concealed the entrance to the caravan. The final turn was due to begin; people returned to their seats; and the chatter subsided. But when silence had been restored except for some whispering, a violent dispute broke out behind the curtain. We could not hear what was being said, but recognized the two voices: that of the tall fellow trying to explain and justify himself, that of the youth reprimanding, angry but at the same time discouraged:

'But, you fool, why didn't you tell me? . . .'

We could not catch any more, though everyone was trying hard enough. Then the voices fell, but the altercation was carried on in low tones until boys in the upper rows began to stamp their feet and cry:

'Lights! Lights! Curtain . . .'

7

THE BANDAGE IS REMOVED

AT last a face appeared – a white face heavily lined, with patches made of sealing wafers stuck on here and there, a face now grinning in elation, now drawn in anguish – and a tall pierrot slid into view like some lay-figure unable to hold itself together, bent over as if suffering from colic, walking on tiptoe as if in fear of unknown dangers, hands entangled in sleeves that swept the ground.

I have no idea what story he was supposed to be miming, if I knew at the time. All I remember is that he was no sooner on the scene than, despite frantic efforts to remain on his feet, he fell down. No sooner up again than down he went – over and over again. Chairs kept getting in his way, four of them at once. In one of his falls he overturned a big table that had been brought into the arena. He ended by sprawling at the feet of the spectators. Two supers, who with some difficulty had been recruited from the audience, dragged him by the feet and after great exertions got him up. Each time he fell he gave a little cry, never quite the same one but always a piteous little cry in which distress and complacency were balanced. The climax was reached when, from a scaffolding of chairs, he tumbled slowly from a great height, uttering a long-drawn-out wail of mingled triumph and despair that drew cries of fright from the women.

During the second part of the pantomime the 'poor pierrot who couldn't stand up' produced from his sleeve – I can't remember why – a little doll stuffed with bran, and with her as partner enacted a scene half tragic, half comic. This culminated in the doll being made to vomit up the entire contents of her body. Then, to the accompaniment of pathetic stifled plaints, he refilled her with something that looked like porridge, and at the moment of greatest tension, when everyone was staring open-mouthed at the unfortunate slimy young personage over whom poor pierrot was moaning, he suddenly seized her by the arm and flung her straight at the head of Jasmin Delouche, whose ear she merely grazed, bouncing off with a splash just under the chin of Madame Pignot. This good lady screamed and recoiled so violently, echoed and imitated by her neighbours, that the bench gave way and the baker's wife, the sad widow Delouche, Fernande, and a score of others went over backwards, their legs in the air, amidst laughter, shouts, and applause. Meanwhile the tall clown arose from the ground, made a deep bow, and said:

'Ladies and gentlemen, we have the honour to thank you.'

It was at this moment, amidst the tumult, that *le grand Meaulnes* who had been silently engrossed throughout the miming, leapt up, grabbed my arm, and pointing to the ringmaster burst out:

'Look! Look at him! I know who he is! Why, of course it's him . . .'

Even without looking, as if for a long while the thought had been hatching in my mind and only needed a peck at the shell to break through, I guessed. By a lamp near the curtain the young stranger was now standing wrapped in a long cape, his bandage removed. In the smoky lamplight, as once before by the dim light of a candle in a room of the château, a silhouette stood out: delicate aquiline features, no moustache. Pale, his lips apart, he was hastily turning the pages of a little red album that might have been a pocket atlas. Except for the scar across his temple which disappeared under the thick hair, he corresponded in every detail with the description *le grand Meaulnes* had given me of the disconsolate lover.

There could be no doubt that he had removed the bandage to let us recognize him. But no sooner had Meaulnes cried out than the young man disappeared into the caravan, though not without having darted towards us a look of connivance and a smile: the smile tinged with sadness with which we were familiar.

'And the other one!' Meaulnes exclaimed. 'Why didn't I recognize him at once! Of course, he's the pierrot of the fête . . .'

He began pushing forwards towards Ganache, but the latter

had already blocked the openings to the arena. One by one the
four lamps had been extinguished, and, stamping our feet with
impatience, we were obliged to follow the crowd moving
slowly in the dim light through the narrow passages between
the benches.

The minute we were outside the tent Meaulnes dashed
round to the caravan, mounted the steps, and pounded on the
door. But it was locked. Apparently the actors behind the red
curtain of the caravan – and in some shelter of their own the
goat, the pony, and the talking birds – had already settled
down for the night and gone to sleep.

8

THE POLICE!

THERE was nothing for it but to join the company making
their way through the dark street towards the schoolhouse. At
last everything was falling into place: the tall ghostly form
Meaulnes had seen on the edge of the wood the last night of
the fête was Ganache, who had taken the desperate youth
under his care and gone off with him. Frantz de Galais had
accepted this nomadic life with its dangers, adventures, and
distractions – it was as though he were beginning his childhood all over again . . .

If until now he had concealed his identity from us and pretended not to know the way to the domain, it was doubtless
because he was afraid of having to go home. But if that was
so, why had he suddenly decided to let us guess the truth
tonight? . . .

Le grand Meaulnes was weighing a dozen projects in his
mind as the crowd slowly dispersed through the village. Next
day was a Thursday, and he decided to go and see Frantz first
thing in the morning. Then the two of them would set out on
the muddy road together, and what a magical journey it
would be! Frantz would explain everything; missing bits of the

puzzle would be fitted in; and the adventure would go on from the point where it had broken off . . .

As for me, I walked through the darkness with a heart too full for speech. Into the broad stream of happiness so many tributaries were flowing: from the mild pleasure of the free Thursday awaiting us backward to the immense discovery we had just made, then forward again to the wonderful opportunities it implied. I recall how, in this spate of generous emotions, I spontaneously held out my hand to the notary's least attractive daughter, a girl to whom I had sometimes been obliged to offer my arm much against my will.

Bitter memories! Still-born hopes . . .

At eight o'clock next morning, our boots and belt-buckles highly polished and our best caps on, we came into the open space before the church. Meaulnes, who had been trying hard not to smile when he looked at me, gave a sharp cry and darted on ahead towards the empty Square. Where the tent and wagons had stood there was nothing to be seen but a broken jug and a heap of rags. The mountebanks had gone . . .

The little breeze that was blowing seemed to us icy. The stones and ruts of the Square seemed to be trying to trip us up. Meaulnes, distraught, made as if to rush off down the road towards Vieux-Nançay, then, on second thoughts, towards Saint-Loup-des-Bois. Then he stood, his hand shielding his eyes, hoping for a moment that our friends had only just gone . . . But which way? In the Square there were several criss-cross wheel-tracks, all of them fading out on the hard surface of the streets. We stood helpless.

And then, as we walked slowly back through the village in the early morning of the Thursday holiday, four mounted gendarmes, tipped off by Delouche the night before, came galloping into the Square, then dispersed through the village to bar all exits, like dragoons on a reconnoitring mission . . . But they were too late. Ganache, the poultry thief, had gone, and his companion with him. The police found no one, neither the thief nor the accomplices who had made off with the capons whose necks he had wrung. Warned by Jasmin's inability to hold his tongue, Frantz must have had a sudden revelation of the commerce that kept them alive when funds in the caravan were low. Filled with rage and shame, he would have mapped out a course and planned to get well away before the arrival of the police. But with no further reason to fear an attempt to make him return to his father's, he had wanted us to see him without the bandage that disguised him, before disappearing.

One puzzle remained: how was it that one and the same man, Ganache, could rob half the village and go to find a nurse for his ailing friend? And yet, wasn't that the poor devil in a nutshell: a thief and a tramp; and at the same time a man with a kind heart?

9

IN SEARCH OF THE LOST TRAIL

As we walked home the sun was dissipating the light morning mist. Housewives stood at the door shaking out mats and gossiping. The fields and woods beyond the village confines were already bathed in the light of the most radiant spring morning I can remember.

On this particular Thursday, senior pupils were expected to appear around eight to put in some extra study: some in preparation for the Certificate of Higher Studies, others with an eye to the Normal School examination. But when we got back – I in low spirits, Meaulnes too bitterly disappointed and restless to settle to any work – the class-room was empty. A ray of sunlight slid over the dust of a worm-eaten bench to pick out the scaly varnish of a planisphere.

How could we possibly stay there in front of a book nursing our disappointment when everything was drawing us out of doors: the birds chasing one another in the branches by the window; the thought of our classmates escaping into the open country; but most of all a feverish desire to explore the part of the route verified by our vagabond guide – the last resource in our nearly empty sack, the one key yet to be tried ... It was more than we could face. Meaulnes paced the room, went to the window, stared into the garden, then crossed to gaze towards the village as if on the watch for someone who would certainly not appear.

'I've been thinking,' he said at last. 'I've been thinking it may not be as far as we imagined . . . Frantz crossed out one whole section of the route I had mapped. That could mean that while I was asleep the mare went a long way round . . .'

I was sitting on the edge of a desk, one foot dangling, staring at the floor, dull and out of sorts.

'And yet,' I argued, 'it took you all night coming back in the Berlin.'

'But we didn't start till midnight! I was put down at four, about six kilometres west of Sainte-Agathe. And I left here by the station road, mind you – that's east. So those two kilometres should be subtracted from the total distance . . . I really believe that once past the Communal wood it can't be more than two leagues to the lost domain.'

'But those are precisely the two leagues that are missing on the map.'

'That's true. And from here to the other side of the wood is a good league and a half. Still, at a brisk pace, it could be managed in a morning's walk . . .'

Just then Mouchebœuf came in. He had an irritating way of passing himself off as a good student, not by working harder than the rest of us, but by making a point of showing up on occasions like this.

'I knew you'd be the only two I'd find here,' he said, very pleased with himself. 'The others have gone off to the Communal, Jasmin Delouche in the lead. He knows where all the nests are.'

Sanctimoniously he began to repeat disparaging things the truants had said about the school, the master, and ourselves when planning their expedition.

'If they're in the woods,' said Meaulnes, 'I shall probably run into them, because that's where I'm going myself. I'll be back around half past twelve.'

Mouchebœuf's jaw fell.

'Aren't you coming, François?' asked Meaulnes, pausing

on the threshold and holding open the door, while into the
stale class-room there came, with a breath of sun-warmed air,
a medley of cries, salutations, chirpings, the sound of a
bucket bumping against the edge of the well, the crack of a
whip in the distance . . .

'I can't,' I replied, though sorely tempted, 'on account of
Monsieur Seurel. But hurry back. I'll be anxious to hear.'

He made a vague gesture and went out quickly, full of
hope.

When Monsieur Seurel put in an appearance around ten he
was wearing, instead of his black alpaca jacket, a fishing coat
with huge buttoned pockets and a straw hat; his trousers were
tucked into short shiny leggings. I doubt whether he was
surprised to find that no one had turned up for work, but he
gave no encouragement to Mouchebœuf who for the third
time was repeating that the truants had said: 'If he wants us,
let him come and get us!'

'Put your books away,' said Monsieur Seurel. 'Get your
caps, and we'll go bird's-nesting for *them*! . . . Can you walk
that far, François?'

I said I could and we set off.

It was agreed that Mouchebœuf should precede Monsieur
Seurel as guide and also as a decoy. He knew the boys would
be searching among some of the tallest trees, and he was to
sing out from time to time:

'Hey! Giraudat! . . . Delouche! . . . Where are you? . . .
Any luck? . . . Found any nests? . . .'

Meanwhile – and this was an arrangement that suited me
perfectly – I was to skirt the eastern edge of the wood in case
the quarry should try to escape that way.

The reason this suited me so well was that on the map as
rectified by our friend – and Meaulnes and I had pored over it
till we knew it by heart – there seemed to be a narrow path,
a mere track, leading away from the wood on that side
in what we assumed to be the direction of the domain. Now
if I could only locate it! . . . And I soon convinced myself
that before noon I should be standing on the road to the lost
manor . . .

And what a marvellous walk it was!... When we had passed the Slope and gone round by the mill I left my two companions: that sneak of a Mouchebœuf, and Monsieur Seurel, who was like someone on the war-path – I even believe he had put an old pistol in one of his pockets.

Taking a cross-path I soon came to the edge of the wood. For the first time in my life I was alone in unfamiliar country, like some patrol with whom the corporal has lost touch.

And now I imagine myself on the brink of that mysterious felicity Meaulnes had one day caught a glimpse of. I have the whole morning to explore the boundary of the wood – the coolest and most secret spot for miles around – and at the same moment my big brother is making an exploration of his own. I follow what must once have been the bed of a brook, under low branches of trees whose name I don't know – they may be alders. A few moments ago I got over a stile at the end of the pathway, to find this stream of green grass flowing beneath the foliage. Now and then I brush against nettles or trample the tall stalks of valerian.

Now and then my foot encounters a patch of fine sand. And in the silence I hear a bird – I imagine it to be a nightingale, but how can it be if they only sing at night? – a bird which repeats the same phrase over and over: the voice of the morning, a greeting that comes down through the leaves, a charming invitation to roam through the alders. Invisible, persistent, it accompanies me on my promenade under a roof of foliage.

For the first time I too am on the path of adventure. For once it is not for shells left stranded by the tide that I am prospecting, with Monsieur Seurel close at hand, nor for specimens of orchis unknown to the schoolmaster; nor even, as so often in old Martin's field, for that deep but dried-up spring protected by a grating and so overgrown with weeds that on each visit it took longer to find... I am looking for something still more mysterious: for the path you read about in books, the old lane choked with undergrowth whose entrance the weary prince could not discover. You'll only come upon it at some lost moment of the morning when you've

long since forgotten that it will soon be eleven, or twelve . . .
Then, as you are awkwardly brushing aside a tangle of branches, your arms at the same time trying to protect your face,
you suddenly catch a glimpse of a dark tunnel of green at the
far end of which there is a tiny aperture of light.

But while intoxicating myself with these hopeful fancies I
emerge, without warning, into a clearing which proves to be
an ordinary field. To my surprise I have reached the far side
of the Communal which had always seemed infinitely remote.
And over there on the right, between two wood-piles, in a
humming, droning pool of shadow, stands the forester's house.
At a window-sill two pairs of stockings are hung out to dry.
Often, in previous years, when entering the wood, one of us
descrying a point of light in the far distance would exclaim:
'There's the forester's house!' But we had never pushed on as
far as that. People would say, as if speaking of some daring
expedition: 'He went all the way to Baladier's!' That was the
forester's name.

This time I had ventured as far as Baladier's myself.

But I hadn't found anything.

My weak leg was beginning to bother me, also the heat
which up to then I hadn't felt. I was dreading the prospect of
going all the way back alone when I heard, quite near, the
voice of Monsieur Seurel's decoy, Mouchebœuf, and then
other voices calling out to me . . .

Some half dozen boys were there, all more or less crest-
fallen except for Mouchebœuf the informer, still pleased with
himself – among them Giraudat, Auberger, and Delage . . .
Thanks to the bird-call some of them had been discovered up
a wild cherry tree which stood by itself in a clearing; others in
the act of robbing a woodpecker's nest. Giraudat, a simpleton
with piggy eyes and a dirty smock, had concealed the nestlings
against his stomach, between his shirt and his skin. Two of
their mates had got away before Monsieur Seurel's arrival on
the scene – probably Delouche and young Coffin. At first they
had responded to Mouchebœuf's signals with injurious
pleasantries, calling him 'Mouche*vache*', an insult which went

echoing through the woods till the victim, stung into a tactical error, cried out:

'You'd better come down out of there! Here's Monsieur Seurel . . .'

With that there was a sudden stillness, then a silent flight through the wood. And as they knew every inch of the ground, pursuit was out of the question. Besides, no one knew which way Meaulnes had gone; his voice had not been heard. Nothing was to be gained by prolonging the search.

It was after midday when we turned slowly back towards Sainte-Agathe, tired, dispirited, and mud-stained. Once out of the wood, as we scraped our boots on the dry ruts of the road, we felt the full force of the sun. The fresh and glistening morning of spring had gone, giving place to the sounds of afternoon. At long intervals we could hear a cock crowing in some lonely farmyard, and it was a mournful sound. Coming down the Slope we stopped to chat with some farmhands who had resumed work after their midday meal. They leaned over a gate to hear the news.

'Young blackguards,' Monsieur Seurel was saying. 'Just look at Giraudat! He's put the fledgelings inside his shirt. They've done what you might have expected – a fine mess, I must say! . . .'

It seemed to me that the farmhands, as they laughed and nodded, were also laughing at my defeat. For that matter they were more or less on the side of the young offenders, most of whom they knew very well. They even confided, once Monsieur Seurel had gone on ahead:

'Another lad went by just now, a tall fellow, you know the one . . . The wagon from Les Granges must have given him a lift part way, because he got down just over there where the lane turns off to Les Granges. He was spattered with mud and his clothes were torn. We told him we'd seen you go by this morning but you hadn't come back yet. He just sauntered off towards Sainte-Agathe . . .'

And in fact when we got to the bridge at the base of the Slope *le grand Meaulnes* was waiting for us, seated on a pier. He looked exhausted. When Monsieur Seurel questioned him he said he too had been looking for the truants. But in answer to my whispered question he shook his head in discouragement and said:

'Not a thing . . . Nothing in the least resembling it.'

After lunch, in the empty class-room, a dark and stuffy prison in a radiant world, he sat down at one of the long desks, and with his head on his arms, disconsolate, fell asleep and stayed motionless for hours. Towards evening, coming out of a long brown study during which he seemed to have reached an important decision, he wrote a letter to his mother. And that is all I remember of the dreary ending of a day of total frustration.

10

WASH DAY

WE were rash to assume that spring had arrived.

On Monday we decided to do our homework immediately after school, as on summer afternoons, and to have a better light we moved two long desks out into the yard. But without warning it clouded over; a drop splashed on an exercise-book; and we scurried indoors. At the wide windows of the dusky school-room we stood gazing up at the grey sky where the wind was playing havoc with clouds in retreat.

Meaulnes, leaning forward with a hand on the window-sash, exclaimed, as if angry at being unable to stem a mounting flood of chagrin:

'Ah, they weren't in quite such a hurry the day I drove down the road in Fromentin's carriole . . .'

'What road?' asked Jasmin.

But Meaulnes ignored him.

To ward Delouche off I broke in: 'What I'd like would be to go for a long drive like that in pouring rain, under a big umbrella . . .'

'Reading all the way,' someone added, 'like in the house.'

'It wasn't raining,' said Meaulnes, 'and I didn't want to read. All I wanted was to look at the countryside.'

But when Giraudat, taking his cue from Jasmin, asked *what* countryside, he too was ignored. And Jasmin said:

'I know . . . He can't get away from that adventure of his . . .'

His manner was conciliating and there was something underlined in his tone of voice, as though he were to some extent in the secret. But it was a waste of time, and his advances met with no response. By now it was getting dark and a cold downpour had set in. One by one the boys pulled their smocks over their heads and made a run for it.

It rained intermittently right up to the following Thursday, which was, if anything, more dreary than the one before. The whole region was veiled in a chilly mist as on the worst days of winter.

Millie, duped by the first sunny days, had had the washing done, but the air had become so damp and cold in the meantime that it would have been useless to spread the sheets out on the hedges of the garden, or for that matter even to hang them in the lofts.

After discussing her troubles with Monsieur Seurel she decided to dry her washing in the class-rooms, as it was Thursday, and proceeded to build up the fire till the stove was red-hot. To economize fuel in the kitchen and dining-room, this stove was to be used for cooking the meals, and we would all spend the day in the main class-room.

When it was first suggested – I was still very young! – the novelty of this arrangement made it seem like a festive occasion.

But the novelty soon wore off. The damp linen absorbed all the heat and it was bitterly cold. Rain fell steadily in the courtyard – the thin soft rain of winter. But after an hour or so, sheer boredom drove me out, and I found Meaulnes in the yard. For a while we stood at the gateway, gazing through the bars towards the high point of the village where the Four-Roads met. A funeral procession was arriving from some distant farm. The coffin was lifted from an ox-cart and set down at the foot of the tall Cross where the butcher had once seen two sentinels on duty. Where was he now, the young captain who had been so proud of his pirates?... The customary rites were being performed: the curé and his acolytes had approached and were now before the coffin. Their lugubrious chanting came faintly to our ears. And I was thinking: this is the one and only event in a day that will trickle away like the sluggish water in the gutter, when Meaulnes's voice startled me out of my moodiness:

'Now I must go and pack. I didn't tell you, Seurel – but I wrote to my mother on Thursday, to ask her to let me finish my schooling in Paris. I'm leaving today.'

His hands pressed high up against the grating, he was still looking away towards the village. No need to ask if his mother had agreed: she was well-off and refused him nothing. There was even less need to ask why he was so eager to get to Paris.

Yet I knew he must be feeling a certain regret, even a kind of fear, at the prospect of leaving Sainte-Agathe which had claims on his affection, if only because it was the starting-point of his adventure. As for me, I was aware of a growing sense of desolation which at the first shock I hadn't felt.

'It will soon be Easter,' he said, and his sigh explained even more than the words.

'As soon as you find her,' I said, 'you'll write and let me know, won't you?'

His hand came down on my shoulder. 'Of course. Aren't you my friend and my brother?'

Slowly I was taking in the fact that it was all over, since he wanted to finish his studies in Paris. Never again should I be standing like this, with my comrade beside me.

The one hope of our being reunited lay in that Paris address which was to provide a clue to the lost trail... But seeing the lines of unhappiness in my comrade's face, I felt it to be a very feeble hope indeed.

My parents were told. Monsieur Seurel was astonished, but at once accepted Augustin's explanations. Millie, a housewife first and foremost, was upset that Madame Meaulnes should find our house draped in damp linen... His box, alas, was all too soon packed. We fetched his Sunday boots from under the staircase, collected his linen from the cupboard, then his books and papers – all the meagre possessions of a youth of eighteen.

At noon his mother drove up in her old-fashioned carriage. She had lunch at the Café Daniel with Augustin and took him off with almost no explanation as soon as their horse had been fed and put back into the shafts. On the threshold we said good-bye; and watched their carriage disappear at a turn of the Four-Roads.

Millie scraped her shoes at the door and returned to the cold dining-room to set things in order again. And for the first time in months I found myself alone before the prospect of a long Thursday afternoon, feeling as though my adolescence had been borne away in that old-fashioned carriage, for ever.

II

I BETRAY MY FRIEND

WHAT was I to do with myself?

The weather had improved a little; the sun was trying to break through.

Somewhere in the house a door banged. Then everything was quiet again. Now and then my father crossed the yard to refill the coal-scuttle, for today the stove was being overfed. I caught a glimpse of white sheets hanging from lines and rebelled at going back to that bleak drying-room only to find myself face to face with the thought of examinations: the Normal School competitive exam. which from now on till the end of the year was to be my one preoccupation.

Yet there was a curious flaw in all this desolation: I felt somehow lighter. Meaulnes gone, and the adventure he embodied brought to its inconclusive end, I was at least free of the haunting anxiety, the mysterious obsession that had hindered me from behaving like everyone else. Meaulnes gone, I was no longer following the footsteps of a visionary pathfinder; I was once more a village lad like the rest of them – a status which demanded no effort and concurred with my own inclinations.

As I stood in the yard undecided, the younger of the Roy brothers went down the street whirling above his head three chestnuts attached to a string. He let go and they flew over the wall and landed at my feet. I was so hard up for something to do that I flung them back, and we kept up this silly little game till, suddenly, he trotted off towards a tumbrel coming up the lane from the Vieille-Planche. I saw him clamber into the back of the cart while it was still in motion. The horse and tumbrel belonged to the Delouches and Jasmin was driving. The bulky form of Boujardon was upright beside him. They were on their way home from the pasture.

'Coming with us, François?' cried Jasmin, who must by now have heard of Meaulnes's departure.

Why not, I thought, and without leaving word at home I climbed into the lurching cart and like the others stood holding on by the side-board. We proceeded towards the inn kept by Jasmin's mother . . .

We are now in a back room of the inn which is at the same time a shop, for the widow also sells groceries. A ray of pale light coming in through a low window gleams on rows of tinned food and casks of vinegar. Boujardon, on the window-sill facing us, is munching Savoy biscuits and when he laughs his fat body shakes like a jelly. The biscuit box is within easy reach, standing on a barrel. Young Roy gurgles with pleasure. A sort of counterfeit intimacy has sprung up among us. I can see that Jasmin and Boujardon are to be my companions from now on; the course of my life has abruptly altered. It seems a long while since Meaulnes went away, his adventure an old story – an unhappy one, but over and done with.

From under the counter young Roy has fished out a bottle of liqueur that has already been opened. Delouche plays the host, but there is only one glass. We drink from it in turns. He serves me first, with a certain condescension, as if I were not used to the ways of sportsmen and farmers. This makes me feel constrained. And as they have begun to speak of Meaulnes, an impulse overtakes me, if only to shed my embarrassment and regain my self-confidence, to show that I know his story, and to reveal part of it. What harm can it do, now that his adventures among us are at an end?...

Have I told the story badly? At any rate it fails to produce the effect I expected.

My companions, like sound citizens who can find an explanation for anything, see nothing in all this to marvel at.

'One of those wedding jollifications,' comments Boujardon.

Delouche saw one at Préveranges which was stranger still.

The château? It should be easy enough to find people who have heard about it.

The girl? Meaulnes will marry her when he's done his military service.

'Why didn't he show one of *us* his map and take *us* into his confidence instead of that actor fellow...'

Entangled now in my lack of success, I feel I must shock them into curiosity. I decide to tell them who the actor fellow really was: where he came from, his whole strange destiny... Boujardon and Delouche are not impressed.

'He's the one who upset everything. But for him Meaulnes wouldn't have been so stand-offish, because when he first came he was just the opposite. And then all that silly business of pirates and night raids, after enlisting us into a sort of school battalion...'

'The more I think if it,' says Jasmin, looking at Boujardon and shrewdly nodding his head, 'the more I'm convinced I did a good job when I tipped off the police. All he did around here was make trouble, and he'd have made a lot more...'

I am almost disposed to agree. Everything might have turned out better if we hadn't made so much mystery about it and taken it so tragically. It was through Frantz that everything had gone wrong...

But the sound of movements in the front room puts an abrupt end to these reflections. Jasmin snatches the bottle and hides it behind a cask. The corpulent Boujardon slides down from the window-sill, knocking over an empty bottle which rolls away in the dust, and he just manages not to sprawl on the floor himself. Young Roy pushes them through the back door in his haste to get away and chokes with laughter.

Without knowing quite why, I join in the flight. We cross the yard and climb a ladder into a hayloft. I hear a woman's voice calling out, 'You good-for-nothings . . .'

'I had no idea she'd be back so soon,' whispers Jasmin.

And it dawns on me that we've been poaching, that we had no right to our biscuits and liqueur. I feel like the shipwrecked mariner who, relieved to find a human to speak to, found himself addressing an ape. My one idea is to get out of the hayloft, for this is the kind of escapade I heartily dislike. Besides, it's getting late . . . They show me a way out through the back, across two gardens, round a duck-pond, and at last I am back in the street full of puddles, in which the lights from the Café Daniel are reflected.

I am not proud of my evening's behaviour. When I reach the Four-Roads I see again, in spite of myself, a hard fraternal face relaxing into a smile – a final wave – and a carriage disappearing round a turning in the road . . .

My smock is flapping in a wind as cold as the wind that blew through all those winter months that were so unhappy and yet so wonderful. And I know now that it is not going to be as easy as I imagined. In the big dim class-room, where they have been expecting me for dinner, sharp draughts disturb the air which in spite of the stove is none too warm. I shiver and let myself be scolded for an afternoon of vagabond-age, without even the consolation of being able to fall into the old routine by sitting down at my own place at the table, for tonight the dining-room is not in use. We hold our plates on our knees, wherever we can find room to sit. In silence I eat the pancake which was to have been a special treat for having to spend this Thursday in the school-room, but the top of the stove was too hot and the pancake is burnt.

Alone in my room I get into bed quickly and try to stifle the remorse which pushes up through all the desolation. But twice during the night I waken: the first time I thought I had heard the other bed creak, as it did whenever Meaulnes turned over, all in one piece; the second time it was his footsteps, as springy and cautious as those of a hunter on the scent, pacing back and forth through the lofts . . .

12

THREE LETTERS FROM MEAULNES

In all my life I've received only three letters from Meaulnes. I have them still, in the drawer of a chest. Each time I re-read them the old sadness comes over me again.

The first arrived two days after his departure.

My dear François,

Today as soon as I got to Paris I went to the address. I saw nothing. There was no one there. No one will ever be there.

The house Frantz spoke of is a little two-storey private one. Mademoiselle de Galais's room must be on the first floor. The windows up there are the ones most hidden by trees, but if you walk along the pavement you can see them quite well. The curtains are drawn and you'd have to be mad to hope that one day between those curtains the face of Yvonne de Galais would appear.

It's on a boulevard. It was raining a little. The trees are green already. You could hear the sharp clang of the trams which kept going by.

For nearly two hours I walked up and down under the windows. There was a wine shop near by where I stopped and had a drink so people couldn't think I was a burglar planning a coup. Then back to the hopeless patrol.

When it got dark, windows all around began to show lights, but not in that house. It is certainly unoccupied. And yet Easter isn't far off.

Just when I was leaving, a girl, or a young woman – I couldn't say which – came and sat on a bench which was damp from the rain. She was dressed in black with a little white collar. She was still sitting there when I went away, in spite of the cold, waiting for heaven knows what, or whom. So, as you see, Paris is full of people as mad as I am.

Augustin.

Time went by. In vain I waited for a line on Easter Monday and the following days – days when, after all the celebrations of Holy Week, there seems nothing to do but wait for summer. June brought with it examinations and a terrible heat wave which smothered the countryside as if in a blanket no breeze could penetrate. Even at night there was not a breath of cool air to relieve the torture. It was during this unbearable month that I received the second letter.

June 189..

My dear friend,

This time all hope is gone. I've known it since last night. The pain, which I scarcely felt at first, now goes on growing.

Every evening I had gone to sit on that bench, watching, imagining, hoping in spite of everything.

Last night after dinner it was dark and stifling. People were out on the street, talking under the trees. Above the dark foliage, green where the light fell on it, second- and third-floor flats were brightly lit up. Some of the windows were wide open. You could see a lamp on a table making a small circle of light in the warm darkness of the June night and revealing almost the whole interior of the room. Ah, if only the black window of Yvonne de Galais had shown a light as well, I think I would have dared to go up, knock, walk in . . .

The girl I mentioned was there again, waiting like me. I thought she might know something about the house and decided to ask her.

'All I know,' she said, 'is that a girl and her brother used to come here during the holidays. But I heard that the brother left his parents' château and they haven't been able to find him. The girl got married. That would explain why the house is shut up.'

I left then. After a few steps I stumbled over a kerb and nearly fell. That night – it was last night – when the women and children in the court were quiet at last and I was hoping for some sleep, I kept hearing the cabs go by in the street. They passed at fairly long intervals, but as soon as one went by I listened for the next in spite of myself: the tinkle of a bell, the clop of hoofs on the asphalt. And the sounds turned into words – the forsaken city, love beyond recall, night without end, summer, fever . . .

Seurel, my friend, I am in great distress.

Augustin.

Letters which after all told me very little. Meaulnes failed to explain why he had remained silent so long and what he meant to do now. I had the impression that he was breaking with me because his adventure was ended, just as he had broken with the past. My efforts to maintain contact were in vain. I received no reply to my letters, except for a line to congratulate me on passing the examinations for the first Brevet. In September I heard from a classmate that he had been to see his mother at La Ferté-d'Angillon during the vacation. But that summer we had spent our own holidays with my uncle Florentin at Vieux-Nançay. And Meaulnes went back to Paris without my being able to see him.

When school reopened I settled down with a sort of grim ardour to prepare for the higher Brevet, in the hope of getting a teaching post the following year without having to attend the Normal School at Bourges, and it was when I was absorbed in study, towards the end of November, that I received the third and last letter.

I still pass by that window. I still wait without a spark of hope. And I know it's mad. These cold Sunday afternoons of autumn, when the light begins to fail, I can never make up my mind to go back to my room and close the shutters for the night till I've been to that bleak street again.

I'm like that crazy woman at Sainte-Agathe who kept stepping outside the front door and gazing towards the station with a hand over her eyes to see if her dead son was coming.

Sitting on the bench, cold and miserable, I keep imagining that someone will take my arm gently . . . I would look round . . . She would say quite naturally, 'I'm rather late.' And all my sorrow and madness melt away. We go into our house. Her furs are cold to the touch; her veil is damp. As she goes in, a taste of the evening mist accompanies her; and as she moves towards the fireplace I see frost glinting in her fair hair, and her profile, so pure and soft, outlined against the flames . . .

But the only light at her window is the dull whiteness of drawn curtains. And even were the girl of the lost domain to open it now, there is nothing left to say to her.

Our adventure is ended. The winter of this year is as dead as the grave. Perhaps when we come to die, death will provide the meaning and the sequel and the ending of this unsuccessful adventure.

Seurel, I asked you one day to think of me. Now I ask just the contrary. It's best to forget me. It's best to forget it all.

A. M.

Then it was winter once more, a winter as dead as its predecessor had been alive with a mysterious life. Everything now was still and empty: the church Square with no sign of strolling players; the school playground deserted at four; the classrooms where I sat before my books alone and listless . . . In February the first snow fell, burying last year's romantic story, confusing the trail, blotting out every last trace. And I tried my best to forget all about it as Meaulnes had asked me to do in his letter.

PART THREE

I

THE BATHING PARTY

To be seen with a cigarette in one's mouth, to put sugar and water on one's hair to make it curl, to snatch a kiss from a schoolgirl wandering down the lane, to jeer at a passing nun from behind a hedge – these were the pastimes of all the bad boys of the village. But bad boys often mend their ways as they grow out of their teens, and turn into quite decent young men. The transition is not quite so simple when the bad boy in question already looks used up and old for his age, when he spends half his time nosing out equivocal information about the women of the village and saying outrageous things about Gilberte Poquelin to make people laugh. Even so there may still be some hope for him . . .

This was the case with Jasmin Delouche. For reasons best known to himself, but certainly with no intention of passing his examinations, he stayed on in the senior course which everyone would have been glad to see him abandon. Meanwhile his uncle Dumas was teaching him his own craft which was that of a plasterer. And soon this Jasmin Delouche, with Boujardon and a quiet lad called Denis whose father was Deputy Mayor, were the only classmates I cared to go about with, and that chiefly because they belonged to 'the Meaulnes era'.

Besides, it was obvious that Delouche did want to be my friend. The truth was that he, who had been Augustin's enemy, would have liked to become *le grand Meaulnes* of the school: at any rate he probably regretted not having been his lieutenant. Less obtuse than Boujardon, I think he missed some element, that touch of the unexpected, that Meaulnes had brought into our life. He would often interrupt the talk with some reference to him:

'Just what *le grand Meaulnes* said one day . . .' or '*Le grand Meaulnes* used to say . . .'

Although he looked like an aged child, Jasmin was more grown-up than we were, and he disposed of resources that greatly enhanced his status: he possessed a dog with a long white coat which, though its pedigree was dubious and its high-flown name 'Bécali' made us wince, was a good retriever of sticks and stones but devoid of other talents. He also possessed a second-hand bicycle which he allowed us to mount in the afternoons unless there were some girl in sight willing to be initiated into this exercise. But his most useful asset was a white donkey which though blind could be harnessed to anything on wheels.

The donkey really belonged to Dumas, but he lent it to his nephew whenever we went to bathe in the Cher. On these occasions Jasmin's mother would contribute a bottle of lemonade which we tucked under the seat among the bathing drawers. Eight or ten of us older pupils would set out, accompanied by Monsieur Seurel, some on foot, some in the donkey-cart which we left at the Grand' Fons farm, as the only way down to the river from there was through a steep gully.

I have reasons for remembering every detail of one such excursion when Jasmin's donkey led the way with our gear and the lemonade and Monsieur Seurel, and we walked behind. It was August. Examinations were over, and released from that nightmare we felt that the summer was ours to make the most of, and we sang without knowing what or why, jubilating in the fine beginning of a Thursday afternoon.

Only one shadow fell across this innocent scene. We caught sight of Gilberte Poquelin walking some way ahead. With her neat figure and her high-heeled shoes she had the provocative air of a girl who will soon be grown-up. She turned off the road into a side-path, no doubt on her way to a farm for milk. Little Coffin suggested that he and Jasmin should follow her.

'Oh,' the latter boasted, 'it wouldn't be the first time I'd kissed her.'

And he launched into some broad stories about her and the girls she went about with while the whole troop of us, out of bravado, wheeled into the side-path, leaving Monsieur Seurel and the donkey to go on ahead. But there was little ardour in the chase and one by one the company fell out. Even Delouche seemed none too anxious to exert his prowess before witnesses, and the girl went on her way, fifty yards in advance. A few crowings, a few whistles, and we turned and made our way back somewhat sheepishly. Once on the road again we had to run to catch up, and the sun was hot. We were no longer singing.

On reaching the bank of the Cher we undressed under the dry willows. They shielded us from prying eyes but not from the sun. Our feet on the hot sand and caked mud, we had visions of the bottle of lemonade, which was cooling in a spring at the Grand' Fons, a spring that bubbled up through the bank of the river. Looking into it you could see the grass waving deep underneath, but its surface was never quite free from two or three insects that looked like wood-lice. But the water was so pure that fishermen never hesitated to kneel down, their hands on either bank, and drink from it.

Unfortunately, today was no exception to the rule . . . For, once dressed and seated tailor-fashion in a circle round the bottle to take our turn at one of the only two tumblers, having politely invited Monsieur Seurel to have first go, there was only enough of the frothy liquid to make each throat prickle and redouble its thirst. So, one after another, we were driven to the contemned spring, lowering our faces cautiously to the surface of the limpid water. But not all of us were experts in out-of-door etiquette. For some of us, I for one, scarcely succeeded in quenching our thirst: either because of a dislike for water as a beverage, or because the fear of swallowing a wood-louse tightened our throats, or because the transparence of the water made it hard to judge the right distance, with the result that faces plunged in and noses were filled with something so icy it seemed to burn . . . Despite these hazards and drawbacks, it seemed to us, on the hot dry bank of the Cher, that all the coolness of the world was imprisoned in this little pool, and to this day when I hear the word 'spring' my mind returns to linger over it.

We set out for home in the dusk, and the first part of the journey was as carefree as before. The lane from the farm to the road was a brook in winter and in summer a ravine full of holes and stumps winding between hedges of tall trees. Some of the party went that way, accepting the difficulties as a challenge. The rest of us, including Monsieur Seurel and Jasmin, took a parallel path, soft and sandy, which skirted a neighbouring field. We could hear the others talking and laughing near us, below us, but invisible in the shadows, while Delouche rattled on with his grown-up stories. In the high branches we could hear a sizzling noise made by night insects and even see them against a sky not yet quite dark as they swarmed round the lacy foliage. Occasionally one would drop and chirrup loudly at our feet. Nothing else broke the calm of the fine summer evening as we sauntered along, unencumbered with hopes or desires, going peacefully home from a banal little outing. It was Jasmin again, though unwittingly, who was to disturb this peacefulness . . .

As we approached the top of the hill where two great stones mark what was said to be the site of an ancient fortress, he began to speak of estates he had visited and particularly of a more or less abandoned domain in the neighbourhood of Vieux-Nançay: a place called Les Sablonnières. With the accent of people from the Allier who have an affected way of clipping certain words and rolling their tongue round others, he told us of having roamed through a ruined chapel there some years back and noticed a memorial tablet on which these words were engraved:

Here lies the Chevalier Galois
Faithful to his God, his King, and his Lady Love

'No, really!' said Monsieur Seurel with a slight shrug. He was a little uneasy at the tone the conversation was taking but did not wish to hinder us from talking like men.

Then Jasmin began to describe the château in question as if he had spent half his life there.

Several times, coming back from Vieux-Nançay, he and Dumas had been intrigued by an old grey turret rising above the firs. And in the heart of a wood they had come upon a maze of ruined buildings where no one was living. One day a local gamekeeper whom they picked up on the road took them through this queer domain. But since then he had heard that the whole place had been razed; that nothing remained but the farm and a small villa. Here the original owners still lived: an old retired officer, now impoverished, and his daughter . . .

He talked and talked. I listened with a growing sense that he was describing something I already knew, when suddenly and quite simply, as so often happens in the case of major revelations, Jasmin turned and touched my arm, struck by an idea that had for the first time crossed his mind:

'But now I think of it – surely that was the place Meaulnes stumbled into – you know, *le grand Meaulnes* – that old story . . .

'Why, of course,' he went on, as I failed to respond, 'I remember now – the keeper did say there was a son, an eccentric young chap with his head full of notions . . .'

I was no longer listening, for I knew he had guessed right. And I knew that, with Meaulnes far away, and all hope abandoned, it was I who had before me, like some familiar well-trodden pathway, the road which led to the domain for which we had had no name.

2

AT FLORENTIN'S

I WHO had always been a dreamy, reserved, unhappy sort of boy turned overnight into what was known among us as a 'decided character' when I saw that the opening of a new chapter in this important adventure depended on me.

And it is from that evening, I believe, that my knee stopped hurting me for good.

Vieux-Nançay was the administrative centre of the commune in which the domain known as Les Sablonnières was situated; it also happened to be the part of the country where

Monsieur Seurel's relations lived. My uncle Florentin had a big general store there, and it was with him that we sometimes spent the latter part of September. But now that examinations were over, I was restive and got permission to go to my uncle's at once. I decided, however, to make no sign to Meaulnes till I was certain of being able to send him good news: to raise false hopes after such bitter disappointments would be worse than cruel.

For years Vieux-Nançay had been the part of the world I loved best, just the place for the last part of the holidays, though we went there less often than I would have liked, and only when there was a carriage to be hired. There had once been a dispute with the branch of the family that lived there, which probably accounted for Millie's reluctance to accept invitations. But bygone family quarrels meant very little to me, and once installed in the midst of a lively lot of uncles and cousins I revelled in a thousand new kinds of fun.

We always stayed with Uncle Florentin and Aunt Julie, who had a son, Firmin, of my own age, and eight daughters, of which the eldest, Marie-Louise and Charlotte, must have been seventeen and fifteen. Their 'universal stores' was situated near one of the entrances to the village, opposite the church, and was patronized by all the landowners and sportsmen of this isolated region of the Sologne, thirty kilometres from the nearest railway station.

The store with its grocery and cotton goods and many other departments had several windows on the main street, and its plate-glass doors gave directly on the Square. But oddly enough – though not unusual in this none too prosperous district – there was nothing in the way of flooring but the beaten earth.

In the rear of the premises there were six rooms, each with its own specialities: one for hats, one for garden tools, another for lamps, and so forth. When as a child I wandered through this bazaar I thought I should never come to the end of so many marvels. Even now, grown into a young man, I felt that holidays spent there were the only ones worthy of the name.

The family lived in a big kitchen which was next door to

the shop – a kitchen where a log fire was always blazing during the last days of September. Here in the early morning sportsmen and poachers who came to sell Florentin their game would accept drinks while the little girls of the house, up already, scurried about and chattered and filled the place with the faint scent of whatever it was they put on their glossy hair. On the walls, faded photographs of school groups revealed my father – it took some time to recognize him in uniform – surrounded by his Normal School classmates . . .

Here we passed the mornings – here and in the yard where Florentin grew dahlias and bred guinea-fowl; where we roasted coffee, seated on soap-boxes; where we prised open packing-cases and unwrapped objects which sometimes we couldn't even put a name to . . .

Throughout the day customers came and went, mostly farmers, often coachmen from the big country houses. In front of the entrance, carts from distant hamlets would be stationed, dripping a little from the early autumn mists. And from the kitchen we listened to the farmers' wives who always had a lot to say . . .

But at night, from eight o'clock on, after we had gone out with lanterns to put hay in the mangers where the horses stood patiently steaming, the whole shop was ours.

Marie-Louise, the oldest girl though one of the smallest, rolling up lengths of cloth and ranging them on the shelves, would call out and invite us to entertain her while she finished her work. Firmin and I and a bevy of girls would invade the big shop where inn-lamps dangled from the ceiling and begin to turn coffee-mills or perform acrobatic feats on the counter. Sometimes we ended by dancing on the smooth clay floor to the music of an old trombone green with verdigris that Firmin had found in the attic . . .

I still blush to think that, during previous holidays, Mademoiselle de Galais could easily have walked in and caught us behaving in such a childish way . . . But it was not until this year, one evening in August just before nightfall, as I was quietly chatting with Marie-Louise and Firmin, that I saw her for the first time . . .

Already, on the evening of my arrival, I had questioned my uncle about the domain of Les Sablonnières.

'It's no longer what you could call a domain,' he had said. 'It was sold, and the people who bought it, for the shooting more than anything else, pulled down the old buildings to enlarge the coverts. What used to be the main court is now overgrown with heather and gorse. The former owners kept nothing but a small two-storied house and the farm. You'll be seeing Mademoiselle de Galais, as she does her own shopping. Sometimes she rides over, sometimes she drives, but in either case it's with the same horse, old Bélisaire – you've never seen anything quite so decrepit.'

I was too moved by all this to ask cold-blooded questions, and yet I wanted to know all he could tell me.

'But they must have been rich,' I prompted.

'Oh yes, Monsieur de Galais was always giving parties to amuse his son – a strange sort of boy with very queer ideas. The old gentleman did what he could to gratify him: invited smart ladies down from Paris, young gentlemen too, from Paris, from all over . . .

'Everything at Les Sablonnières was going to rack and ruin, Madame de Galais hadn't much longer to live, and still they tried to keep him amused and gave in to all his whims. It was only last winter – no, the winter before – that they gave their biggest fancy-dress fête. Half the guests were from Paris, half from the neighbourhood. They bought or hired hundreds of splendid costumes – they had contests, races, boats . . . all to amuse Frantz de Galais. They said he was going to be married, and the fête was to celebrate the engagement. But he was much too young. And suddenly the whole thing fell to pieces. He went off, and nobody's seen him since . . . The lady of the château died, and Mademoiselle de Galais found herself there alone with her father. He was at one time an officer in the Navy.'

'You mean she isn't married?' I asked at last.

'No, not that I've heard of. Why, have you got views in that direction?'

Disconcerted, I told him as discreetly as possible that my best friend, Augustin Meaulnes, might have.

'Well,' said Florentin with a smile, 'if he doesn't mind taking a wife without a fortune he couldn't do better . . . Would you like me to speak to Monsieur de Galais? He comes in now and then to buy buckshot. I always give him a glass of my oldest home-made brandy.'

Hastily I begged him not to mention the subject, but to wait. And I thought it wiser to wait myself before sending word to Meaulnes: to wait at least until I had seen the girl myself. For there was something unsettling about so many fortunate auguries.

I hadn't long to wait. Next evening, just before dinner, it began to grow dark and a cool mist came up, more like September than August. Taking advantage of a moment when the shop was free from customers, Firmin and I went in to talk to Marie-Louise and Charlotte. I had confided in them my reason for coming to Vieux-Nançay ahead of time. Leaning on the counter or seated on it with both hands spread out flat on the polished wood, we exchanged what facts we knew about the mysterious young lady, which didn't amount to much after all, when a sound of wheels made us look up.

'Here she is now,' whispered one of the girls.

A few moments later a strange equipage drew up in front of the glass doors: an outlandish old farm wagon with rounded panels and moulded ornaments; an aged white horse with head bent so low that he seemed to be hoping to find grass in the road; and in the driving seat – I say it in the simplicity of my heart, well knowing what I say – perhaps the most beautiful young woman that ever existed in the whole world.

Never had I seen such charm united with such seriousness. Her dress revealed the slenderness of her waist – slender to the point of fragility. She got down slowly and came into the shop, removing a brown cloak from her shoulders – the most serious of girls, the most fragile of women. A mass of fair hair made a frame for her forehead and face, which was finely outlined and finely modelled. On her clear complexion the summer sun had placed just two freckles. In so much that was beautiful I was to find only one flaw: in moments of sadness or discouragement or merely of pensiveness, her face would be faintly streaked with red, as happens in the case of persons harbouring some grave illness which has not yet made itself known. At such moments admiration gave place to a kind of pity, all the more poignant for being so unexpected.

These were the impressions I formed as she came towards my cousins and began to talk to Marie-Louise, who at length introduced me.

Someone brought forward a chair and she sat down, back to the counter, while we remained standing. She was quite at home in the shop and seemed to like her surroundings. My Aunt Julie had been sent for and stood talking sensibly, like the peasant-shopkeeper she was, her hands folded over her stomach, her head under a white cap nodding sagaciously, and this delayed the moment – which intimidated me a good deal – when I should be drawn into the conversation.

But nothing could have been simpler.

'And so,' said Mademoiselle de Galais, 'you'll soon be a schoolmaster.'

My aunt lit a chinaware lamp hanging over our heads and it shed a dim light over the shop. Looking at the childlike features, the candid blue eyes, I found it hard to reconcile them with the decision and earnestness in the tones of her voice. When she stopped speaking her eyes would turn away and remain fixed on some distant object as she waited for a reply, and she had a habit of half biting her lip.

'I would teach too,' she said, 'if my father weren't opposed to the idea. I should like to teach the little boys, like your mother . . .' And she smiled, as if by way of acknowledging that my cousins had spoken about me.

'You see, with me the village people are always polite, and kind, and helpful. And I'm really fond of them – though for that matter why shouldn't one be? . . .

'But their attitude towards the schoolmistress is, don't you think, rather mean and cantankerous? They're for ever complaining that penholders have got lost, or the exercise-books cost too much, or the children aren't learning anything . . .

I feel sure I could cope with their antagonism without losing their goodwill. Though of course it might not be easy . . .'

And she fell once more into her childlike attitude, her blue eyes thoughtful and unsmiling.

The easy way in which she could pick up a delicate subject and put into words subtleties that one usually finds only in books made the three of us feel awkward and tongue-tied, and there was a moment of silence before the talk was resumed.

Then with a hint of regret, or possibly of revolt against conditions too private for us to know about, the young lady went on:

'But most of all, I would teach those boys to be sensible. I'd impress upon them a kind of wisdom I do know something about. I wouldn't fill their heads with a desire to go roaming about the world, as you will probably do, Monsieur Seurel, once you're an instructor. I'd teach them how to find the happiness which, if they only knew it, is within easy reach . . .'

Marie-Louise and Firmin were as much taken aback as I was. We could find nothing to say. She guessed our embarrassment, stopped, bit her lip, lowered her eyes, and then with a smile, as if making fun of us:

'And so, for all we know, some tall young man, a little mad, may be roaming far and wide in search of *me*, while I sit here under the lamplight in Madame Florentin's shop, keeping my old horse waiting at the door. If that young man saw me, the chances are he wouldn't believe his eyes, don't you agree? . . .'

Her smile gave me the hardihood to say, for it was time to say it and I tried to lighten the words with a laugh:

'Perhaps I know this tall young man who is a little mad.'

She looked up quickly.

But there was a tinkle at the door and two women came in with baskets on their arms.

Aunt Julie turned to her guest as she pushed open the kitchen door. 'Won't you step into the "dining-room"? You can talk in peace there.'

Mademoiselle de Galais declined and rose to take leave when my aunt added:

'Monsieur de Galais is here. He's having a talk with Florentin by the fire.'

There was always, even in August, a fire in the big kitchen, and logs of fir were now flaring and crackling. There, too, a china lamp was lit and I saw an old man with a mild face, his cheeks hollowed and clean-shaven, a man who had little to say and seemed overwhelmed by years and memories. He and Florentin were seated before little glasses of *marc*.

'Ah, François!' my uncle shouted in his hawker's voice, as if there were a river or several acres of ground between us, 'I've been planning an outing by the Cher for next Thursday – with shooting, fishing, dancing, bathing . . . We'll be expecting you too, Mademoiselle; Monsieur de Galais is agreed. You're to ride over. It's all settled . . .

'By the way, François,' he added, as if he had just thought of it. 'You might bring that friend of yours, Monsieur Meaulnes – that was the name, I think you said.'

Mademoiselle de Galais got up, suddenly very pale. And only then did I remember that Meaulnes, that day in the strange domain, near the lake, had told her his name . . .

When she held out her hand to me before leaving, there was between us, more clearly than if it had been expressed in words, a secret understanding that only death was to bring to an end, and a friendship more moving than a great love.

At four next morning Firmin knocked at the door of the little room assigned to me in the yard where the guinea-hens lived. It was still dark and I fumbled for my things on a table littered with brass candlesticks and brand-new plaster saints chosen from the shop on the eve of my arrival to embellish the apartment. Out in the court I could hear Firmin pumping air into the tyres of my bicycle. In the kitchen Aunt Julie was puffing at her fire. The sun was just coming up as I set out. But I had a long day ahead of me: I was going by way of Sainte-Agathe to have lunch and explain my protracted absence, and I hoped to arrive at La Ferté-d'Angillon in time to spend the evening with my friend Augustin Meaulnes.

3

AN APPARITION

I HAD never made a long journey by bicycle – this was the first. But Jasmin had given me secret lessons some time ago, and in spite of my bad knee I had learned how to ride. If an athletic youth can take pleasure in the possession of such a machine, how much more did it mean to one who after half an hour's walking would begin to drag a leg behind him in sweating misery! And now, to swoop down from a hill-top into the hollows as if on wings; to see a blurred landscape far ahead divide and make an aisle for you and burst into leaf as you passed; to slip through a village taking everything in at a glance . . . Only in dreams had I been wafted on such delightful flights. Even the hills failed to daunt me – after all, what could possibly be distasteful to me on a road that led to the village of my friend!

'Just before you get there,' Meaulnes had once told me, 'you'll notice a huge metallic wheel with flat-boards to catch the wind.' He didn't know what it was used for, or perhaps pretended not to know in order to whet my curiosity.

It was not until late in the afternoon that I caught sight of the big wheel turning in the breeze above a broad meadow, doubtless pumping water for the neighbouring dairy-farm. Beyond a row of poplars bounding this meadow the outskirts of the village came into view. As the road curved away to follow the course of a brook, the scene opened out more and more until from a bridge the village lay before me on both sides of its main street.

Cows were grazing in the meadows, half hidden by reeds; I heard their bells as I dismounted and stood holding the handle-bars of the bicycle while my eyes roved over the tranquil scene into which I was bringing such disturbing news. The houses, linked to the road by small wooden bridges like gangways were lined up on the edge of the ditch bordering the road; they might have been little ships with sails furled, moored there for the night. It was the hour when in every kitchen fires were being lighted.

As I stood there, fear, or rather a kind of reluctance to break in on such peacefulness, began to drain away my assurance. This sudden faltering was aggravated by the recollection that my Aunt Moinel also lived in La Ferté-d'Angillon where she had a house in a little Square.

She was in fact a great-aunt. All her children were dead, but I had known the youngest quite well: Ernest, a tall youth who was going to be a teacher. His father, my great-uncle Moinel, formerly town clerk, had died soon after him. And my aunt now lived alone in an odd little house full of patchwork rugs. On every table there were cats, hens, and cocks made of paper; on the walls hung old diplomas, portraits of people long since departed, and medallions made of their hair.

Amidst these lugubrious mementoes she was bizarre good humour personified. When I had found the little Square where she lived I called out through the front door which stood half open and heard her exclaim in her high-pitched voice from the last of three rooms that opened one into the other:

'Good gracious! Good gracious!'

She upset some coffee on the stove – why on earth should she be making coffee at this time of day? – and then she appeared. Standing very erect, shoulders thrown back, she wore on her head something which was at the same time cap, bonnet, and hood. Perched high above her large protuberant forehead, it gave her the look of a Mongolian or a Hottentot. She kept breaking into little peals of laughter which revealed what remained of her small, pretty teeth.

While I was hugging her she reached quickly, awkwardly for one of my hands. And in a mysterious manner which was rather pointless, since we were quite alone, she slipped into my hand a small coin which I didn't dare look at but guessed to be a franc. Then, as I hesitated between thanking her and asking for an explanation, she patted my shoulders and said:

'Take it! I know what it's like.'

She had always been poor, always borrowing, always spending.

In her sharp falsetto, but quite cheerfully, she would say: 'I've always been stupid, and always unlucky.'

Taking it for granted that a lack of pennies was at the basis of my preoccupations as it was of her own, the kind old lady hadn't waited for me to take breath before pressing upon me what was left of the day's household money. And from that time on, this was the way she always welcomed me.

Dinner was no less strange – half pathetic, half bizarre. She kept a candle within reach and at one moment would remove it, leaving me half in darkness, or at another place it on a small table covered with chipped or cracked plates and vases.

'The handles of this one,' she said, 'were smashed by the Prussians in '70. Because they couldn't take it with them.'

And it was that vase with its tragic history that reminded me of a night some years before when we had dined and slept in this house. My father was taking me into the Département of the Yonne to consult a specialist about my knee. We were to catch a through train that stopped at La Ferté before daybreak . . . I recalled that dismal meal and the long-winded stories of the old town clerk as he sat with his elbows on the table before a bottle of pink-coloured wine.

I also remembered how frightened I had been that night. For after dinner, in front of the fire, Aunt Moinel buttonholed my father to tell him a story about a ghost: 'I turned round . . . And ah! my poor Louis, what did I see? A little woman all grey . . .' Her head was chock-full of such terrifying nonsense.

And this night too, after dinner, when tired from the day's exertions I had put on a checked nightshirt that had once been worn by my great-uncle and got into bed in the big room, she came to sit beside me and began in her most mysterious and most high-pitched tone:

'My poor François, I must tell you something I've never told a soul . . .'

'Just my luck,' I thought. 'She'll scare me out of another night's sleep, like ten years ago . . .'

But I listened. She looked straight ahead, and kept nodding, as if she were telling the story to herself:

'I was on the way home from a fête, with Moinel. It was the

141

first wedding we'd been to, together, since poor Ernest died. My sister Adèle was there. I hadn't seen her for four years. An old friend of Moinel's – he's very rich – had invited him to the wedding of his son, at a place called Les Sablonnières. So we hired a carriage – it was quite an expense too. We were driving back and it was about seven in the morning, in the middle of winter. The sun was just coming up. Absolutely no one for miles around. When suddenly, what do I see ahead of us, on the road? A little chap, a young man, very short and very handsome. He stood in the middle of the road, waiting for us to come up with him. Soon we could see his face – a face so white and so pretty that it was frightening . . .

'I clutched at Moinel. I was trembling like a leaf. I thought it was the Good Lord Himself! . . . And I whispered to Moinel: "Look!" I said. "An apparition!" . . .

'He was furious with me.

' "Be quiet, you old chatterbox!" he said. "I can see him as well as you."

'He didn't know what to do. Then the horse stopped . . . Close to, you could see how pale the poor thing was, with a forehead bathed in perspiration – wearing an old beret, long trousers . . . Then a very sweet voice said:

' "I'm not a man, I'm a girl. I've run away, but I can't go any farther. Would you let me ride with you?"

'So we told her to get in. But no sooner in the carriage than she went off in a faint. And you'll never guess who she was. She was the fiancée of that young man I was telling you about at Les Sablonnières, Frantz de Galais, where we had been invited for the wedding.'

'But there wasn't any wedding,' I said, 'since the fiancée ran away!'

'It's true,' she said, looking at me wistfully, 'there was no wedding. And all because the poor girl had got a lot of foolish ideas into her head. She told us all about it. Her name was Valentine, and she was one of the daughters of a poor weaver. She had made herself think that such happiness was not for her, that the boy was far too young, that he had made up all the wonderful things he described to her, so that when the time came for Frantz to go and fetch her she took fright. He walked with her and her sister in the garden of the Archbishop's palace at Bourges, in spite of the cold and the wind. The young man, out of sheer politeness, because it was the younger sister he was in love with, showed some attention to the older one. And so this poor mad creature of mine began imagining things. She said she was going in to get a shawl, and then, to throw them all off the scent, she put on men's clothes and started off on foot along the Paris highway.

'Her fiancée got a letter saying she'd gone to meet another man she was in love with. And there wasn't a word of truth in it . . .

' "I'm happier," she told us, "at having made a sacrifice for him than if I were his wife." Yes, poor deluded child, but he never had the faintest intention of marrying her sister! What he did was to put a bullet through his brains. They saw blood in the woods, but they never found the body.'

'And what did you do with the poor girl?'

'First we made her take a sip of brandy. Then we gave her some food, and when we got home we made her a bed near the fire. She spent a good part of the winter here. All day long, till the light went, she sewed and made clothes and trimmed hats and helped with the housework, she was at it from morning to night. It was she who mended that upholstery you see over there. Since her stay here the swallows nest out of doors. But in the evenings, when it got dark, her day's work done, she would make some excuse to slip out into the yard or the garden or the street, even when it was so cold it split the stones. And we'd find her there, crying her heart out.

' "There, there," I'd say. "Tell me what it is!"

' "It's nothing, Madame Moinel."

'And she'd come in again. The neighbours said:

' "You've found a very pretty little maid, Madame Moinel."

'We begged and implored, but she was set on going to Paris, and in March she went. I gave her some dresses she had made over, and Moinel bought the railway ticket and gave her a little money.

'She didn't forget us either. She's a dressmaker now in

143

Paris, near Notre-Dame. She wrote to us and always asked for news of Les Sablonnières. So once and for all, to set her mind at rest, I wrote and told her the domain was sold and everything pulled down, that the young man had gone away for good, and his sister had got married. For that matter, I think it's the truth. Since then my Valentine hasn't written as often as she did . . .'

If it was not a ghost story that my aunt Moinel had told me in the strident little voice so well adapted to such tales, it was none the less extremely disturbing. For one thing we had sworn to Frantz the vagabond that we would be as brothers to him, and here, if ever, was the occasion to prove it . . .

And yet, was this the moment to cloud all the happiness in store for Meaulnes by telling him what I had just learned? What sense would there be in launching him on another wild-goose chase? It's true we had the girl's address, but where in the world was our vagrant by this time? . . . Madmen, I argued, should be left to their own mad devices. Delouche and Boujardon were not so far off the mark: we had suffered enough at the hands of the capricious Frantz. And I made up my mind to tell Augustin nothing until I had seen him safely married to Mademoiselle de Galais.

This decision out of the way, I was still oppressed with a presentiment of misfortune. But I told myself this was absurd and drove it from my mind.

The candle was guttering. A mosquito buzzed. But my aunt, her elbows on her knees, her head bent forward under the velvet hood which she never took off till she went to bed, had begun her story all over again . . . Every little while she would look up to see what impression it was making on me, or possibly to see if I was still awake. Finally, driven to it, I lay back, closed my eyes, and pretended to drowse.

'But I see you're sleepy,' she said in a tone of faint disappointment.

I was sorry for her and protested:

'Not at all, Aunt, I assure you . . .'

'Oh, but you must be. Besides, I can't expect you to be interested in stories about people you never heard of . . .'

And this time I was coward enough not to reply.

4

I BRING THE NEWS

NEXT morning as I turned into the main street, the fine holiday weather, the great tranquillity, and the familiar stirrings of a village coming to life at the beginning of a new day restored my confidence – after all, wasn't I the bearer of good tidings? . . .

Augustin and his mother lived in the former schoolhouse. On the death of his father, who, enriched by a legacy, had been living in retirement for some years, Augustin had wished to buy the school where the old man had taught for twenty years and where he himself had learned to read. Not that the big square building presented a very amiable appearance: it looked in fact like a town hall, and that is what it had been. The windows of the ground floor were placed so high from the street level that no one ever looked out of them; and the yard at the back, treeless and bounded by a high roofed-in shelter, which shut off any view of the surrounding country, was grimmer and more arid than any deserted playground I had ever seen . . .

In the passage, on which four doors opened, I met Madame Meaulnes coming in from the garden with a big basket of washing which she had apparently hung out to dry in the first hours of this long holiday morning. Wisps of grey hair escaped from her old-fashioned bonnet, and her face with its regular features was swollen and tired as if she had spent a sleepless night. Her head was bent and she seemed to be brooding rather unhappily.

But on seeing and recognizing me she smiled:

'Ah, you've come just in time. He's going away. I spent the night doing his accounts and getting his things together. The train goes at five, but I expect we'll have everything ready in time . . .'

From her manner it might have been assumed that she herself had decided the whole thing, yet she probably hadn't the least idea where Meaulnes was off to.

'Do go up,' she said. 'You'll find him in the Mayor's office. He's writing.'

I hurried upstairs and opened a door on the right which still bore a plate marked 'Town Hall' and found myself in a big room with four windows, two on the side of the street and two overlooking the fields. On the walls were faded portraits of former Presidents of the Republic – Grévy and Carnot. A platform ran the whole length of the far wall and on it stood a baize-covered table and the chairs once occupied by members of the Council. In the mayoral arm-chair sat Meaulnes dipping his pen in an old-fashioned porcelain inkwell in the shape of a heart. It was in this setting, more suited to some retired functionary, that Meaulnes spent the long vacation, when he was not roaming the countryside . . .

As soon as he saw who it was he got up, but not with the alacrity I had anticipated.

'Seurel!' he exclaimed, as if astounded – and that was all he said.

It was the same tall figure, the same bony face and close-cropped head. An untidy moustache was beginning to straggle over his lips. His look was as straightforward as ever, but something like a veil of mist dimmed the ardour of the old days, except at rare moments when a flash of his former intensity would dispel it . . .

He seemed quite put out at seeing me there. At one bound I had reached the platform, but to my surprise he didn't even think of holding out his hand. He had turned towards me, his hands behind him, and he was leaning backward against the table, with an air of acute embarrassment. He was in fact looking at me without seeing me, as if considering what to say. Always one to weigh his words, slow to begin speaking, like men who live alone – hunters, explorers – he would take a decision without a thought for the words in which it could be

146

formulated. And now that I stood there before him, he had to think up as best he could some phrases that would provide an explanation.

Meanwhile, with as much light-heartedness as I could assume, I told him how I had got there, where I had passed the night, how surprised I had been to find his mother preparing for his departure . . .

'Ah! She told you?'

'Only that you were going away . . . I suppose it's just a short trip somewhere.'

'No. A very long one.'

Disconcerted, but feeling sure that in a moment I should be saying the word that would nullify his plans, whatever they were, I was for the moment tongue-tied and couldn't think how best to broach the subject of my mission.

But he had begun at last to speak, and it was in the tone of a man trying to justify himself.

'You know, Seurel, what that strange adventure meant to me, during that time at Sainte-Agathe. It was my one reason for living, my only hope in the world. With that hope gone, what was there left? How could I just go on living like everyone else? . . .

'However, I did try to, in Paris, when I saw that it was all over and there was no further point in looking for the lost domain . . . But how can a man who has once strayed into Heaven ever hope to make terms with the earth! What passes for happiness with most people seemed contemptible to me. And when I tried, deliberately and sincerely, to live like the rest of them, I stored up enough remorse to last me a very long time . . .'

Seated on a chair by the table, staring at the floor, listening, but not looking at him, I could make nothing of such a veiled explanation.

'But Meaulnes,' I said at last, 'do speak more plainly. Why this long journey? Is it something wrong you've done that has to be put right? Or some promise you have to keep?'

'Well, it is really. You remember that promise I made to Frantz . . .'

147

'Ah!' I interrupted in great relief. 'If that's all it is . . .'

'Not only that. There may also have been a "wrong" to be put right. The two go together . . .'

In the silence that followed I made up my mind to speak and was thinking how to begin when he went on:

'There's only one way I can explain it. Of course I should have liked to see Mademoiselle de Galais once more – just to see her . . . But I'm sure now that when I discovered the nameless domain I was at some peak of perfection, of purity, to which I shall never again attain. Only in death, as I once wrote you, can I expect to recapture the beauty of that moment . . .'

Then with a new note in his voice and a strange animation he said, coming nearer to me:

'But listen, Seurel! This new project, this long journey, the wrong I've done which must be redeemed, in a way it's only a continuation of that former adventure . . .'

He paused, as if painfully trying to put his memories in order. I had let one opportunity slip. I was determined not to miss another, and I spoke – too hastily, and later I was to regret most bitterly not having waited to hear his confession first.

I therefore came out with the words I had been rehearsing – words adapted to the situation of a few moments ago, but not to the present one. Quietly, and scarcely glancing up at him, I said:

'And if I were to tell you that all hope is not lost? . . .'

He looked at me, then turning abruptly away, blushed as I've never seen a man blush before or since: a deep flush that must have pounded at his temples.

At length he said, in a voice so low I could scarcely hear him:

'What do you mean?'

So then, from beginning to end, I told him all I knew, all I had done, and how, now that the whole situation was altered, it was as if Yvonne de Galais herself had sent me to him.

He was now deathly pale.

He had been listening in silence, his shoulders slightly hunched, in the attitude of a man caught unawares, trying to defend himself, or hide, or escape. Only once, I remember, did

148

he interrupt me. I was speaking of the demolitions at Les Sab-lonnières and said, almost in parentheses, that the domain as he had known it no longer existed:

'There you see!' he exclaimed, as if he had been waiting for a chance to justify his conduct and the despair into which he had sunk. 'You see – there's nothing left . . .'

Feeling sure that any remaining scruples would be swept aside by the facilities we had provided, I concluded my account by telling him about the picnic party my uncle Florentin had got up. I said that Mademoiselle de Galais would be riding over, that he himself was invited . . .

But he seemed completely adrift, and said nothing.

'And so,' I said, growing impatient, 'this trip of yours will have to be cancelled. We'd better go and tell your mother.'

On the stairs he hesitated a moment, then said:

'You really think I ought to go to that picnic?'

'Well, naturally – what a question!'

He was like someone you have to push by the shoulders.

When we got downstairs Augustin told his mother that I was staying for lunch, for dinner, and for the night, and that he planned to hire a bicycle and ride back to Vieux-Nançay with me next morning.

'Yes, of course,' she said, nodding her head as if this was exactly what she had foreseen.

I sat down in the small dining-room whose walls were ad-orned with illustrated calendars, daggers, and ornate leather bottles which an uncle of Augustin's had brought back from the Sudan where he had served with the marines.

Augustin excused himself for a moment before lunch and went into the next room where his mother had prepared his luggage. And I heard him tell her in undertones not to un-pack his trunk, as his journey might only be postponed . . .

5

THE OUTING

IT was hard to keep up with Augustin on the road to Vieux-Nançay, for he rode like a racing cyclist and even pedalled up the steep hills. His unaccountable hesitation of the previous day had given place to a nervous, feverish desire to push on that made me a little fearful. At my uncle's he showed the same impatience and seemed unable to fix his attention on anything until at ten next morning we were all seated in the carriage, ready to set out for the banks of the river.

It was late in August and summer was nearing its end; already the white road was strewn with the empty yellowing shells of fallen chestnuts. We had not far to go. We were to meet at the Aubiers farm near the Cher, some two kilometres beyond Les Sablonnières. From time to time we came up with other guests in carriages, and even young fellows on horseback whom Florentin had made bold to invite in Monsieur de Galais's name. As on a previous occasion, invitations had gone out to rich and poor alike, men of property and peasants. It was therefore no surprise to see Jasmin Delouche cycling along the road. My uncle had made his acquaintance some time before through Baladier, the forester.

'And to think,' remarked Meaulnes as he caught sight of Jasmin, 'that *he* of all people had the clue, while we were hunting as far afield as Paris!'

Each new glimpse of him seemed to increase his rancour. Delouche, on the contrary, preened himself on having earned our gratitude and made a point, like a faithful escort, of riding as close to our carriage as he could. He had taken pains to spruce himself up, but the results were rather lamentable, I thought, watching the skirts of his shabby jacket flapping against the mudguard of his bicycle . . .

Despite a dogged amiability his young-old face inspired anything but liking, and I began to feel sorry for him. But for whom was I not to feel sorry before the day was ended . . .

I can never recall that outing without an obscure feeling of regret and of constriction. I had so looked forward to it! Everything seemed to conspire towards a happy outcome. And so little happiness resulted . . .

And yet what could have been lovelier than the banks of the Cher on that bright morning! We drew up at the foot of a gentle declivity which overlooked a panorama of green meadows and groves of willow with a criss-cross of hedges dividing the scene into what might have been a collection of little private gardens. From the opposite bank grey hills rose steep and rocky, and on the horizon, among patches of woodland, one caught glimpses of small châteaux with romantic turrets. Far away, at intervals, one could hear the baying of hounds belonging to the château of Préveranges.

We had made our way down through a maze of narrow lanes full of white pebbles, or sand – lanes which springs turned into brooks as they neared the river's edge. We caught our sleeves on the thorns of wild gooseberry bushes. At one moment we plunged into the cool shade of a ravine, and a moment later, at a point where the line of hedges was broken, came out into the full clear sunlight which shed a radiance over the whole valley. Across the river a man sat on a rock patiently angling. Never was there a more beautiful day.

Near a group of birches we sat down on the grass: it was as smooth as some vast lawn, with plenty of room for games.

The horses had been unharnessed and led to the Aubiers farm. Under the trees we began to unpack hampers of food, and on the grass we set up the folding tables and chairs which my uncle had provided.

Then it was suggested that someone should be stationed at the junction of the roads to show late-comers how to reach the site we had chosen. I volunteered, and Meaulnes came with me. We took up our post near the suspension bridge, at a point where several paths converged, including the one which led to Les Sablonnières.

To pass the time we walked up and down, talking of old times. Another carriage from Vieux-Nançay came into sight, bringing country people unknown to us, among them a tall girl with fluttering ribbons. Another long wait, until a donkey-cart came ambling along. In it were three children whose father had formerly been a gardener at Les Sablonnières.

'I seem to recognize them,' said Meaulnes. 'I think it was those two who took my hand that night, the first night of the fête, and showed me the way to the dining-room . . .'

At that moment the donkey decided to go no farther, and the children got out to pull and push and beat him with all their might. Meaulnes, disappointed in them, pretended he had mistaken their identity . . .

I asked them if they had seen Monsieur or Mademoiselle de Galais on the road. One said he didn't know. Another said he thought so. Which got us no farther.

They went off at last towards the picnic ground, pulling at the bridle and pushing the cart from behind, and we resumed our watch. Meaulnes gazed towards the turning of the road to Les Sablonnières, watching with dread the approach of the very person he had once searched for so ardently. A strange, almost comical irritation had taken possession of him, and he took it out of Jasmin. From the top of a mound we had climbed to have a wider view of the road, we could see Delouche down there on the broad patch of green among a group, taking the centre of the stage.

'Look at the idiot showing off!' said Meaulnes.

'What of it! Poor chap, he doesn't mean any harm.'

But Augustin was not to be mollified. As we watched, a hare or a squirrel must have run out from a thicket. Jasmin, as if his prestige required him to make some gesture, pretended to chase it.

'Bravo! Now he's sprinting!' said Meaulnes, as though this were the crowning insolence.

This time I couldn't help laughing. Meaulnes too, but only for an instant.

Another fifteen minutes went by.

'She may not be coming after all,' he said.

'But she promised. Do try to be patient.'

Again he gazed down the road. But after a while he could bear the tension no longer.

'Listen, François. I'm going back to the others. I don't know what there is about me at the moment, but I feel that if I stay here she'll never appear – I just can't believe I shall be seeing her in a few minutes coming down that path . . .'

He went off towards the grounds and left me alone. To kill time I walked along the path to Les Sablonnières a hundred yards or so, and then, at the first turning, I saw her, riding side-saddle, and for once the old white horse was so cheerful that she had to hold him in to prevent him from trotting. At the horse's head Monsieur de Galais was walking with difficulty. No doubt they had taken turns on the way, walking and riding.

When she saw me alone she smiled, dismounted quickly, handed the reins to her father, and came towards me as I ran to meet her.

'I'm glad there's no one but you,' she said, 'for I don't like to make an exhibition of my poor Bélisaire nor put him among other horses. For one thing he's so old and ugly; and then I'm always afraid he'll be kicked and injured. He's the only horse I dare mount; so when he's gone I shall never ride again.'

As with Meaulnes, I detected beneath this charming poise and vivacity a hint of impatience and almost of anxiety. She was speaking a little faster than usual, and in spite of the heightened colour of her cheeks, there was around her eyes and on her brow an extra pallor which betrayed an inner turmoil.

We decided to hitch the horse to a tree in a coppice near the roadside. The old gentleman, taciturn as always, took a halter from a saddle-pocket and proceeded to tie the horse – rather too close to the ground I thought. I promised to have a feed of hay and oats and some straw sent over from the farm . . .

And Mademoiselle de Galais walked towards the picnic ground as, I imagine, she walked towards the shore of the lake when Meaulnes saw her for the first time.

One hand through her father's arm, the other drawing aside the light cloak she wore over her frock, she moved towards the group with the childlike gravity that was so much a part of her character. I walked at her side. All the guests, scattered about or playing games, looked up and drew together to greet her and stopped talking as she came near.

Meaulnes stood among a group of young men and there was not much to distinguish him from his companions except that he was taller than most of them. He did nothing to draw attention to himself, made no gesture, took no step forward – I saw him there, in his grey suit, motionless, gazing like all the others at the arrival of this girl whose beauty was so striking. At last, however, in a gesture half unconscious, he passed his hand over his head, as if he were embarrassed to be seen, among so many well-combed young fellows, as close-cropped as any rustic labourer.

Mademoiselle de Galais was now surrounded. Young people she didn't know were being introduced. In a moment it would be the turn of my friend, and he could not be more unnerved than I was. I was on the point of making the introduction myself. But before I could speak she turned towards him with a surprising self-assurance:

'Ah, there's Augustin Meaulnes,' she said, and held out her hand.

6

THE OUTING

CONCLUSION

OTHERS pressed forward to greet Yvonne de Galais and the pair were separated. By an unlucky chance they were not placed at the same table when it was time for lunch. But Meaulnes seemed to have recovered his assurance and good spirits. I found myself isolated between Delouche and Monsieur de Galais, and two or three times during the meal, when I caught Augustin's eye in the distance, he made me a friendly signal.

It was only towards evening, when most of the party were playing games, bathing, rowing on the Aubiers lake, or talking together that Meaulnes was again face to face with Mademoiselle de Galais. He had joined Delouche and me, and we were seated on garden chairs we had brought with us, when she broke away from a group of young people with whom she seemed a little bored and came towards us. She asked, I remember, why we were not on the lake.

I said we had been rowing earlier in the afternoon but it was monotonous and we had got tired of it.

'Then why not try the river?'

'The current is too strong; we might get carried away.'

'What we should have,' said Meaulnes, 'is a motor-boat or a steam-boat, as we had once before.'

'It's not there now,' she said, almost in a whisper. 'We sold it.'

There was an awkward silence, and Jasmin took this opportunity to go in search of Monsieur de Galais.

'I think I know where to find him,' he said, and walked away.

Oddly enough these two persons, so utterly unlike, had taken to one another at sight and had scarcely been separated all day. Monsieur de Galais had even drawn me aside to say that in Jasmin I had a friend full of tact and deference and abilities. For all I knew he had even confided in Delouche the existence of old Bélisaire and his place of hiding.

I, too, was wondering whether I should not withdraw, but the other two seemed so ill at ease, so uncertain with one another that it seemed wiser to stay . . .

But all Jasmin's discretion and all my prudence were of little avail. They did talk. But fatally, with an obstinacy of which he was certainly unaware, Meaulnes kept going back to the past and all its marvels. And at each evocation the tortured girl could only repeat that everything had vanished: the strange and complicated old house pulled down; the lake drained and filled in; the children and all their gay costumes dispersed . . .

'Ah!' Meaulnes sighed, in despair, and it was as though each item in the catalogue of disappearances added fresh evidence in the case he was arguing against the girl, or against me . . .

We were walking side by side . . . In vain I tried to steer the talk into a channel that might dispel the gloom settling down over all three of us. But once more, abruptly, Meaulnes returned to his obsession. He plied her with questions about everything he had seen at the domain: the little girls, the driver of the old Berlin, the racing ponies . . .

'Have they been sold too? You mean there are no horses left on the place?'

She could only reply that there were none. She said nothing about Bélisaire.

Then he spoke of the objects in his room: the candlesticks, the big mirror, the broken lute; he enumerated them with an irrelevant intensity, as if determined to make sure that no trace whatever subsisted of his wonderful adventure, that this girl was unable to produce a single bit of wreckage to prove they hadn't both been dreaming, like a diver who brings up a mere handful of seaweed and stones from the depths of the sea . . .

Mademoiselle de Galais, like me, couldn't help smiling, sadly. Then she tried to explain:

'You'll never again see the fine château Monsieur de Galais and I tried to make agreeable to poor Frantz . . .

'We spent our life trying to meet his wishes. He was such a strange creature, and such a charming one. But everything went from us the night of his broken engagement.

'My father was already ruined, though we didn't know it at the time. Frantz had made debts and his creditors, former friends, put in their claims as soon as they heard of his disappearance. It reduced us to poverty. My mother died, and within a few days we had lost all our friends.

'If Frantz is still alive, if he were to come back and find his friends again, and the girl he loved, if the marriage were to take place after all, perhaps things could be as before. But can the past ever be revived?'

'Who knows?' said Meaulnes, thoughtfully. And he asked no more questions.

We were walking almost without a sound over a carpet of turf already turning yellow. Augustin had at his side the girl he had thought lost to him for ever. When he asked one of his callous questions her lovely face would turn slowly towards him, and she would look up at him with troubled eyes. Once she laid a hand on his arm gently, in a gesture of trust and helplessness. Why was *le grand Meaulnes* at that moment like a stranger, like a man who has failed to find what he sought and for whom nothing else held any interest? Three years before such a gesture would have overjoyed him to the point of terror, perhaps even of madness. Why then this present emptiness, this aloofness, this inability to be happy?

We were nearing the coppice where that morning Monsieur de Galais had hitched his horse. The setting sun lengthened our shadows on the grass. From the distance came a cheerful humming of the voices of people playing games and little girls laughing, and we remained silent in the midst of a wonderful tranquillity. And then, from the other side of the little wood, from the direction of the farm by the lakeside, we heard a voice singing. It was a man's voice, young, and some distance away – probably someone taking the cattle to be watered. The rhythm was that of a dance tune, but the singer drew it out sentimentally, giving it the nostalgic intonation of some old ballad:

> I've got on red shoes . . .
> Lover, good-bye!
> I've got on red shoes . . .
> For-ever, good-bye!

Meaulnes had lifted his head and was listening. It was one of the airs sung by the belated peasants on the last night of the fête when the disintegration had already set in, another memory, and the most discordant, of wonderful days that would never return.

'Listen . . . Do you hear?' he was saying, in a low voice. 'I must go and see who it is.'

He turned quickly away and walked towards the direction from which the singing came, making straight for the little wood that lay between. Almost at once the song came to an end. As the singer moved farther away he could be heard whistling to his cattle, then silence . . .

I glanced at my companion. Pensive, and disheartened, she

kept her eyes fixed on the coppice through which Meaulnes had disappeared. How often, in days to come, would she look in the same melancholy way towards the wood through which *le grand Meaulnes* would have disappeared, for ever.

'He's unhappy,' she said sorrowfully. 'And perhaps I can't do anything for him.'

I hesitated to answer, fearing that Meaulnes, who must have reached the farm very quickly and already be on his way back, would find us discussing him. Yet I meant to encourage her: to say she must not be afraid of offending him; that he was certainly tormented by some secret which of his own free will he would never confide to her or to anyone – when we heard a cry from the other side of the coppice. It was followed by a sound of stamping hoofs and neighing, then voices in sharp altercation . . . I was certain that something had happened to old Bélisaire and hurried towards the scene of the commotion. Mademoiselle de Galais followed me at a distance. From the picnic ground our movements must have been noticed, for as I entered the thicket I heard the cries of people who came running.

The old horse, tied too low, had got one leg entangled in the tether. He had remained standing quietly until Monsieur de Galais and Delouche, in the course of their stroll, approached. Then, possibly because of the oats to which he was not accustomed, he became excited and tried to break away. The two men had tried to free him but had gone about it so clumsily that he was more entangled than ever, and their efforts were impeded by the fear of being kicked by the frightened animal. It was at this moment that Meaulnes, returning from the farm, came upon them. Furious at such incompetence, he brushed the two men aside at the risk of sending them sprawling in the bushes. Cautiously, but with a few swift movements, he got the horse free. Too late, for a tendon must have been strained or a bone broken, judging from the way the animal stood trembling, head down, one leg drawn up under him. The saddle had slid half-way down, and he was a pitiable object to look at. Meaulnes was leaning over the injured limb but said nothing.

When he looked up there were several of us standing round in a circle. But he saw no one. He was livid with rage.

'Who the devil hitched him like that? And left his saddle on all day! For that matter whoever had the nerve to saddle a horse that's hardly fit even for the shafts!'

Delouche was trying to speak, to take the blame on himself . . .

'You hold your tongue,' said Meaulnes. 'It's all your fault. I saw you yanking stupidly at the halter – as if that would free him! . . .'

He bent down again and rubbed the injured tendon with the flat of his hand.

Monsieur de Galais had said nothing till now and it was a pity he could not have remained in the background. Drawing himself up, he stammered out:

'Naval officers are not in the habit . . . My horse . . .'

'Oh, so it's *your* horse!' Meaulnes cut in, more calmly, as he looked at the old man, his face flushed.

I was expecting to hear a change in his tone, even an apology. But he was breathing hard, and I saw that he took a sort of bitter despairing pleasure in aggravating the situation, in smashing everything once and for all, as he added with calculated scorn:

'Then all I can say is, I can't congratulate you.'

Someone suggested:

'Perhaps cold water . . . if you stood him in the ford . . .'

Again Meaulnes interrupted. 'There's only one thing to do, and that's to get the poor beast home while he can still stand on his legs – and there's no time to lose – then put him in the stable and keep him there.'

Several young men at once offered to help, but Mademoiselle de Galais quickly thanked them, and with her cheeks on fire, holding back her tears, she bade everyone good-bye, including Meaulnes who, quite out of countenance, stood there not daring to look at her. She took the animal by the reins as one holds a friend by the hand, more as if to make contact with him than to lead him . . . The late summer air was mild; it was more like May now than August, and in the breeze that blew from the south the leaves of the hedges quivered . . . We watched her move away, one arm held out from the cloak draped over her shoulders, her slim hand grasping the heavy leather reins. Her father walked haltingly by her side . . .

And that was how the day ended. Baskets, plates, knives, and forks were collected, chairs and tables folded and stacked. One by one carriages and wagons drove away, laden with bundles and passengers. Hats were lifted, handkerchiefs waved. At length only we two were left, with uncle Florentin who like us was ruminating his great disappointment in silence.

And then we drove away, at a brisk pace, in our well-sprung carriage drawn by a splendid young bay. At a point where the road turned off, the wheels grated on sand and Meaulnes and I, seated facing the back, soon lost sight of the entrance to the cross-road where old Bélisaire and his masters had turned off . . .

Then without warning my companion – who of all the inhabitants of the globe I would have thought the least capable of weeping – turned towards me a face broken up by an irresistible onrush of tears.

He placed a hand on Florentin's shoulder.

'Stop the carriage, please . . . Don't bother about me. I'll walk back.'

With one hand on the sideboard he sprang down, and to our stupefaction, turning his back on us, he began to run, and ran all the way to the cross-road we had just passed: the path to Les Sablonnières. It would take him to the avenue among the firs where, a lost vagrant, he had hidden behind the low-hanging branches and listened to some charming unknown children holding a mysterious conversation . . .

And it was that evening, in a voice broken by sobs, that he asked Mademoiselle de Galais to marry him.

7

THE WEDDING DAY

IT is a Thursday in early February, a clear, icy afternoon with a strong wind blowing. It is half past three – or four. In the villages washing which has been spread out to dry on the hedges since noon is flapping in the wind. In each house a fire in the dining-room throws a sheen over varnished toys set out as if on an altar. Tired of playing, a child sits beside his mother listening to the story of her wedding day . . .

For a man who prefers not to be happy, there is the attic where he can listen till nightfall to the creakings and groanings of shipwrecks, or the open road where the wind will blow his scarf against his mouth like a sudden kiss that brings tears to the eyes. But for one who loves happiness there is a house by the side of a muddy footpath, the house at Les Sablonnières, the door of which has just closed on my friend Meaulnes and Yvonne de Galais, who became his wife at noon . . .

Their engagement lasted five months. It was a tranquil time, as tranquil as their first meeting had been the reverse. During that time Meaulnes made many visits to the house, sometimes driving over, sometimes cycling. Two or three times a week as she sat sewing or reading by the big window overlooking the moorland and the woods, Mademoiselle de Galais would catch sight of his tall silhouette passing quickly before the curtains as he arrived by the roundabout route which had first brought him to the domain – but this was the only allusion – and a tacit one – that he made to his memories. His unaccountable torment seemed to have been subdued by happiness.

One event which made history for me but caused no great stir during these peaceful five months was my appointment as schoolmaster in the hamlet of Saint-Benoist-des-Champs, for you can hardly call it a village. It comprises a few scattered farms, and the schoolhouse stands alone on a hill-side near the road. I live a solitary life there, but if I take a short cut through the fields I can be at Les Sablonnières in three-quarters of an hour.

Another change is that Delouche is now living at Vieux-Nançay with his uncle, a master-mason. In due course he will take over the business. He often comes to see me. Meaulnes, at the request of his fiancée, now shows him more friendliness.

And this explains how he and I happen to be wandering about the place at four o'clock, now that the other wedding guests have all gone home.

The ceremony, a very quiet one, took place at noon in the old chapel of Les Sablonnières which was left standing and which is half hidden by firs on the side of the hill. After a simple lunch Madame Meaulnes, Monsieur Seurel and Millie, Florentin, and a few others drove away. Jasmin and I stayed behind . . .

We walk along the edge of the wood which stretches away behind the house. On one side of us is an expanse of waste land where the château and its outbuildings formerly stood. Without admitting it we are extremely uneasy, although we could not say why. As we stroll aimlessly on, we try to throw off our anxiety by pointing out the tracks of hares, or their lairs, or patches of sand recently scratched by rabbits . . . here and there a snare . . . the footprints of a poacher . . . but we keep turning towards the edge of the woods for another sight of the house which seems so silent and impenetrable . . .

In front of the large window overlooking the firs there is a wooden balcony half buried in weeds which sway in the wind. On the window-panes there is a dull glow cast by a fire within, and now and then a shadow moves across it. All round – in the fields, the kitchen garden, the farmhouse – sole relic of the former outhouses – life is at a standstill. The tenants have gone off to the village to celebrate the wedding of their young masters.

Now and then the wind, damp with enough mist to moisten our cheeks, brings the sound of a piano, like some tune gone astray. I stop to listen. The music coming from the depths of the inscrutable house is at first like some far-away tentative

162

voice intimidated by an excess of joy, or the laughter of a child who has gone to fetch all her toys and spread them out before a new playmate . . . It is also like the timorous, questioning regard of a woman who has put on her finest gown but is not sure it will find favour . . . This melody, which I've never heard before, is a kind of prayer to happiness, an entreaty asking fate not to be too cruel, a salutation to happiness and at the same time a genuflexion . . .

I say to myself, 'They are happy at last. Meaulnes is there at her side.'

To know that, to be sure of it, is enough to fill me with contentment, simple child that I am.

Absorbed in these thoughts, my face wet as if spattered with sea-spray by the wind blowing over the moor, I feel a hand on my shoulder.

'Listen!' Jasmin whispers.

I look round at him. He makes a sign not to move, and stands still, his head forward, frowning, straining his ears . . .

8

A SIGNAL FROM FRANTZ

'Hou-ou . . .'

This time I hear it too. It is a cry I've heard somewhere long ago: a prolonged call, one high note followed by a lower one. And suddenly I recognize it: the cry of the tall mountebank outside the school gateway signalling to his young companion. It is the appeal which Frantz had made us swear to respond to, whenever or wherever we might hear it.

But what brings him here today, this young trouble-maker!

'The cry came from the plantation of firs on our left,' I say in a whisper. 'It's probably a poacher.'

Jasmin shakes his head. 'You know very well it's not.'

Then, in an undertone:

'They've both been hanging about here all day. At eleven

o'clock I came across Ganache in a field near the chapel. He was spying. When he saw me he made off. His back was splashed with mud as if he'd come a long way by bicycle . . .'

'But what can they want here?'

'How should I know? Anyhow we'll have to chase them away. With them prowling around the place it'll be the same crazy business all over again.'

Without admitting it, I feel sure he is right.

'The best thing,' I suggest, 'would be to have a talk with them, find out what they're up to, and make them see reason . . .'

So with great caution we make our way forward, crawling through the underbrush towards the deep wood from which we still hear, at intervals, the prolonged call which, though not in itself sinister, fills us both with foreboding.

It is difficult to advance into the heart of this part of the woods without being seen, for there is a wide opening between the evenly spaced firs. As we cannot hope to take them by surprise, I post myself at one corner of the wood, Jasmin goes to the opposite corner. Now each of us has a view of two sides of the rectangle it forms, so that neither of the pair can get away without being seen and hailed. Then from my observation post I play the role of a scout offering a truce and call out:

'Frantz . . .

'Frantz . . . There's nothing to be afraid of . . . It's me – Seurel . . . I want to speak to you . . .'

A few moments of silence. I am about to call out again when, from the depths of the forest, too far for me to see, someone calls out an order:

'Stay where you are. He'll come to you.'

Gradually I make out through the tall tree trunks, which at a distance seem close together, the young man's silhouette. As he comes nearer I see that he is shabbily dressed and spattered with mud. His trousers are held in at the ankle by bicycle clips. An old midshipman's cap is jammed down over hair which has grown too long. His face is thinner – he looks as if he'd been crying . . .

164

He walks boldly towards me, and in an arrogant tone demands:

'What do you want?'

'It's not what I want, Frantz, but you. What are you doing here? Why must you upset people who are happy? What do you want here? Say what it is.'

As if taken off guard, he blushes, falters, then blurts out:

'Well, I'm not happy . . . I'm so unhappy . . .'

Leaning against the trunk of a tree, his head buried in his arms, he begins to weep bitterly. We've gone a few steps into the wood. Here there is complete silence. Not even the voice of the wind can get through the tall firs bordering the wood. And through the avenues of trees nothing can be heard but the rise and fall of his stifled sobs. I wait for the crisis to pass, then with a hand on his shoulder:

'Come with me, Frantz. I'll take you to them. They'll welcome you like a child that was lost and has been found again, and your miseries will be at an end.'

Nothing I could say would move him. In a voice hoarse with tears, wretched, stubborn, wrathful, he broke out:

'So Meaulnes has thrown me over! Why doesn't he come when I call? Why doesn't he keep his promise?'

'Look here, Frantz! The time has gone by for all that abracadabra; we're grown-up people now. Your caprices will only upset the happiness of those you love: your sister and Augustin Meaulnes.'

'But he's the only one who can save me, and you know it. Only he can find the trace. For nearly three years Ganache and I have travelled the length and breadth of France, searching, searching . . . The only chance left was your friend. And now he won't answer my call. He's found the one he lost; why can't he think of me now? He's simply got to take to the road. Yvonne will let him go – she's never refused me anything.'

He turned towards me a face on which the tears had made rills through the dirt, the face of an exhausted and defeated child. There were freckles under his eyes; his chin was badly shaved; his hair straggled over a dirty collar. Hands in his pockets, he stood there shivering. He was no longer the young prince in rags of days gone by. At heart no doubt he was more of a child than ever: imperious, whimsical, and suddenly deflated. But it was hard to accept such childishness in a youth already showing signs of age . . . At one time he had been so alive with arrogant youthfulness that one could condone any folly. Now one began by pitying him for having made such a botch of his life and ended by irritation at the role he still insisted on playing: the young hero of romance. Moreover, I couldn't help thinking that our handsome young Frantz so lyrically in love must have been reduced to theft for a living like his partner Ganache . . . All that arrogance – and now this . . .

Meanwhile I had been thinking it over. 'If I promise you,' I said finally, 'that within the next few days Meaulnes will do as you ask and set out on this search . . .'

'He will be successful, won't he?' he interrupted, his teeth chattering. 'You're sure of that?'

'I should think so – with him nothing is impossible.'

'But how shall I know? Who's to tell me?'

'Come back in a year's time – the same place, the same hour. You'll find the girl you love.'

I made this promise fully resolved not to risk bringing trouble into the life of the newly married young people. My plan was to follow up the information my aunt Moinel had given me and set about finding the girl myself.

He was looking at me with a naïve and total confidence. Fifteen years old! He was still only fifteen – the same age as when he helped to sweep out the school-room at Sainte-Agathe, the same age as when he exacted from us that puerile, terrible oath.

Then the old dejection came over him, for there was nothing left to say except:

'Very well. We'll go away.'

He glanced round at the familiar scene, and it must have been with a twinge of regret at having to leave it again.

'In three days' time we shall be on the road to Germany. We left our wagons some distance away. It took us thirty hours without stopping to get here. We wanted to arrive in time to take Meaulnes away before the wedding and get him to help us. We thought if he had found his domain he could also find my fiancée . . .'

Then as he turned to go he said, with a return of his dreadful puerility:

'Call back that Delouche of yours, because if I come face to face with him there'll be trouble.'

His grey silhouette grew smaller and at last vanished behind the firs. I called to Jasmin and we were resuming our watch when we caught sight of Augustin who was closing the shutters of the big window. There was something in his attitude that arrested us.

9

IN THE HOUSE

LATER I came to know in detail all that happened in the course of that day at Les Sablonnières.

Early in the afternoon Augustin and his wife, whom I still call Mademoiselle de Galais, were left alone in the sitting-room. When the guests had gone Monsieur de Galais set out for Vieux-Nançay, whence he was to return at dinner time to give orders at the farm and lock up for the night. As he was leaving, the door remained open a moment letting a cold draught blow through the passages.

And now the house is immune from the outside world, of which the only reminder is the scratching sound made against a pane by the leafless branch of a rose-bush. Like passengers on a boat adrift, the lovers, in the wintry gale, are enclosed in their own happiness.

'The fire is getting very low,' said Mademoiselle de Galais, and moved towards the wood-box.

Meaulnes quickly intervened and placed a fresh log on the embers.

Then he took the hand she held out to him and they stood

167

there facing one another, as if made silent by an event too full of meaning for words.

The wind swept by with the sound of a river in spate. Now and again a drop of rain struck a window-pane, leaving a slanting streak, as on the window of a train.

At length she left his side and crossed to the door, turning to give him a mysterious smile before going out into the passage. For a few moments, in the room full of shadows, Augustin remained alone. The ticking of a small clock reminded him of the dining-room at Sainte-Agathe. He may have been thinking: 'Am I really in the house that was lost for so long, with its secret corridors and whisperings . . .'

It must have been at that moment – for Mademoiselle de Galais told me later that she too had heard it – that Meaulnes heard the first call from Frantz, quite close to the house.

That was why, when the door opened again and the young woman came in with an armful of souvenirs, it was in vain that she spread them out before him: dolls she had once played with; old photographs, of herself dressed up as a tiny *vivandière*, of herself and Frantz on their mother's lap – and such a pretty mother . . . a few dresses she had kept for years, including 'this one which I must have worn just before you knew me, about the time you first arrived at Sainte-Agathe . . .' Meaulnes saw and heard nothing.

Only for a moment did he appear to be aware once more of his wonderful, unimaginable happiness:

'You're there,' he said softly, as if just to say it were intoxicating. 'You move near the table and your hand rests on it a moment . . .'

And then:

'When my mother was still a young woman, she used to lean forward slightly, the way you do, to tell me something . . . And when she sat at the piano . . .'

Mademoiselle de Galais offered to play for him before night came on, but it was dark in the corner where the piano stood and they had to light a candle. The rose-coloured shade made even more vivid the flush on her cheeks which betrayed a great anxiety . . .

It was then, as I stood at the edge of the wood, that I must first have heard the quivering music borne to us on the wind and so soon disturbed by the second call of the two madmen approaching us.

Meaulnes went to the window and stood for some time looking out while she played. Now and then he would turn and gaze at the gentle face, so apprehensive and so defenceless. At last he walked over to the piano and put his hand on her shoulder. She felt, close to her throat, the light weight of this caress and knew there must be some way of responding to it.

'It's getting dark,' he said. 'I'll close the shutters. But don't stop playing.'

Who can say what obscure forces were then at work in a heart that had never been tamed? I was to ask myself that question over and over before I knew the answer – and then it was too late. Some secret remorse? Some unaccountable sorrow? Fear of seeing this incomparable happiness slip away from his grasp? And in that case, some terrible temptation to smash at once, and irrevocably, this rare treasure he had won . . .

He went out slowly, silently, after a final glance towards his young wife. From the edge of the wood we saw him close one leaf of the shutters cautiously, with a vague glance in our direction, then close the other, and a moment later he was running rapidly towards us. Before we could think of taking cover, and just as he was about to leap over a low hedge which had recently been planted along the side of a field, he caught sight of us. At once he changed course. I recall his haggard face and hunted look . . . He made as though to retrace his steps and cross the hedge farther down, near the little brook.

I called out:

'Meaulnes! . . . Augustin . . .'

He paid no attention. Then, convinced that nothing else would check his flight, I cried:

'Wait! Frantz is here.'

Then he stopped. Panting, and without giving me time to think what I should say, he exclaimed:

'Where is he? What does he want?'

'He's very unhappy . . . He came to ask for help – in his search . . .'

'Ah!' He stared at the ground, 'I thought it was that . . . I tried to drown the idea, but it's no use . . . But where is he? Tell me – quickly.'

I said that Frantz had left and there was certainly no chance of overtaking him now. At this Meaulnes seemed greatly vexed. He hesitated, took a few steps, stopped . . . He seemed lost in the depths of chagrin and indecision. I told him what I had promised the young man in his name, that I had made a rendezvous in a year's time . . .

Usually so self-controlled, Augustin was now in an extraordinary state of impatience and agitation:

'Why, oh why did you do that! . . . He was right, I probably *can* save him. But it simply can't wait. I must see him, and talk to him. I must ask his pardon, and do what I can to put things right again . . . Otherwise I can never go back there . . .' And he looked away towards the house.

'You mean,' I said, 'that you're ready to ruin your happiness for the sake of a childish promise?'

'Oh, if it was merely that . . .'

So there was, after all, some other link between the two. What it might be I couldn't imagine.

'In any case,' I argued, 'it's too late to go running after them. They're on their way to Germany.'

He was about to reply when Mademoiselle de Galais appeared before us, pale, dishevelled, her dress torn. She must have been running, for her face was bathed in perspiration. And she must have fallen, for there was a scratch on her forehead just over her right eye, and blood under her hair.

I have sometimes seen, in the more squalid streets of Paris, police engaged in trying to separate a man and a woman whom until then the neighbours had assumed to be a happy, united, respectable couple. Without warning a violent quarrel has broken out, perhaps at the moment of sitting down to a meal, or just before a Sunday promenade, or in the midst of a child's birthday party . . . and in a second the whole place is in an uproar: the man and woman have turned into demons while their children hurl themselves between them, crying, clinging, imploring . . .

Mademoiselle de Galais, when she reached Meaulnes's side, reminded me of one of those poor terrified children. I am sure that if all her friends, a whole village, the whole world had been looking on, she would still have come running, dishevelled, weeping, stumbling, splashed with mud.

But when she made certain that he was there, that for the moment at least he was not abandoning her, she passed a hand through his arm and smiled through her tears like a child. Neither of them spoke. But as she reached for a handkerchief Meaulnes took it from her and gently wiped away the blood that was staining her hair.

'Come,' he said. 'We'll go in now.'

I watched them walk away with the strong wind of a winter evening whipping their faces, he guiding her over the rough ground – she smiling and eager – towards the house that had for a moment been deserted.

10

FRANTZ'S HOUSE

ANYTHING but reassured, oppressed by fears which the happy outcome of last night's turmoil could not dispel, I had to spend the day shut up in the schoolhouse. Immediately after the study period which followed the afternoon lessons I set out for Les Sablonnières. Night was drawing in when I reached the avenue through the firs, and the shutters were already closed. I didn't like to intrude at such a late hour on the day after a wedding, and for some time roamed about the grounds in the hope of seeing someone come out of the house. But no one appeared. Even at the farm nothing seemed to be stirring. I ended by turning homewards, full of sombre imaginings.

Next day, a Saturday, brought the same uneasiness. When school was over I quickly took down my cape and stick, got some bread to eat on the way, and reached Les Sablonnières just at nightfall, to find the house shut up as before. A light was showing upstairs, but I heard nothing, saw no one . . . I walked towards the farmyard and could see through an open door that a fire was burning in the big kitchen. It was time for the evening soup, and I heard voices. This was comforting but not informative, and I couldn't very well make inquiries in that quarter. So I returned to my sentry-go, hoping in vain that the door would open and reveal the tall figure of my friend . . .

Not until Sunday afternoon did I summon up courage to ring the door-bell at Les Sablonnières. On my way across the fields, as I climbed to the top of a bare hillock, the sound of distant bells came to my ears – ringing for Vespers. On this wintry Sunday I felt lonely and sad, weighed down by dread. So I was not unduly surprised when, in answer to my ring, Monsieur de Galais himself came to the door and told me that Yvonne was ill with a high fever, that Meaulnes had been obliged to leave on Friday for a long voyage, that no one knew when he would be back . . .

The old man, worried and embarrassed, did not invite me in, and I took leave at once.

When the door closed behind me I stood on the steps for a moment bewildered, a tight feeling at my heart, and stared idly at the dry twig of a wistaria as it swayed mournfully in a ray of thin sunshine.

So the secret remorse which Meaulnes had been nursing ever since his return from Paris had at last got the better of him. In the end my friend had felt obliged to break away from a happiness that constricted him . . .

Every Thursday and every Sunday I rang the door-bell to ask how Yvonne de Galais was progressing, until the evening when she felt well enough to see me. I found her seated before the fire in the sitting-room whose big window overlooked the heath and the wood. Instead of being pale as I had expected, she was hectic, with bright red patches under her eyes; and her manner was nervous in the extreme. Although she still seemed very weak she was dressed as if to go out. She spoke little, but with great vivacity, as if trying to persuade herself that all chance of happiness was not yet gone . . . I have no recollection of what was actually said until I nerved myself to ask when Meaulnes would be back.

'I don't know,' she said quickly.

In her eyes there was an entreaty, so I asked no more questions.

I went to see her often. We would sit chatting by the fire in the low sitting-room where it seemed to grow dark earlier than anywhere else. She never spoke of herself and her secret sorrow. But she never tired of asking about the days when we were class-mates at Sainte-Agathe.

She would listen gravely, tenderly, almost maternally to detailed accounts of our trials and hardships as grown-up boys. None of our childish exploits, even the boldest and most dangerous, seemed strange to her. This gentle sympathy and understanding, which she got from her father, had not been exhausted even by her brother's follies. The one thing with which she reproached herself, I believe, was not having been a sufficiently intimate confidante, since Frantz, in the moment of his great defeat, had not dared to be more open with her than with anyone else, but had passed sentence on himself as one hopelessly lost. And, when one thinks of it, what grave responsibilities she had assumed: a dangerous one in condoning the extravagant fantasies of her brother; a crushing one in linking her destiny with that of an adventurous spirit like my friend *le grand Meaulnes*.

That she was still loyal to her brother's boyish caprices, that she still tried to preserve some vestiges of the dream-world he had lived in up to the age of twenty, I know from a most touching proof she gave me one day – I might almost say a most mysterious proof.

It was an evening in April, as bleak as late autumn. For nearly a month we had been enjoying a false spring, and she had begun to resume the long walks she had liked to take with her father. But on this occasion the old man was tired and she had asked me to go with her in spite of a threatening sky. And in fact, over half a league from the house, as we walked by the shore of the lake, we were overtaken by showers of rain and hail. We found shelter in an open shed and stood there close together, pierced by the cold wind, looking out over the blackened landscape, thinking our own thoughts. I see her now, dressed with almost austere simplicity, extremely pale, secretly tormented.

'We must go back,' she was saying. 'We've been gone so long. Who knows what may have happened!'

But to my surprise when we ventured out from our shelter, instead of turning back towards Les Sablonnières, she continued in the direction in which we had been walking. I followed, and after some time we came to a house I had never seen before, standing quite alone beside a disused track which must have led towards Préveranges. It was a small house with a slate roof and nothing to distinguish it from the usual type of unpretentious dwelling in that part of the country except its remoteness and isolation.

From her manner one would have thought that the house was ours, and that we had left it unoccupied while away on a long journey. She leaned over to open a little gate, then hurried forward to make an inspection of the desolate scene. We were in a grass-covered yard now ravaged by the storm, where children must have been playing during the late winter afternoons. A hoop lay in a puddle. In little beds where children had planted flowers and peas the heavy shower had left mere streaks of white gravel. And when we came up to the house itself we found, huddled against one of the rain-soaked doors, a brood of young chickens, drenched and miserable. Most of them were dead under the stiffened wings and bedraggled feathers of the hen.

With a stifled cry of pity Yvonne de Galais stooped down, ignoring the puddles and the mud, and separated the live chickens from the dead ones, placing them in a fold of her coat. Then she produced a key and we went into the house. Four doors opened on a narrow passage through which the wind came whistling. She opened the first on the right and showed me into a room where after adjusting my eyes to the dim light I saw a large mirror and a small bed covered, country style, with an eiderdown of red silk. She left me for a few moments and went off to explore the other rooms, coming back with her patients now nesting in a down-lined basket. This she carefully placed under the eiderdown. A lingering ray of sunlight – the first and the last of the day – filtered into the room, making our faces even paler and the growing twilight even murkier, as we stood there in the strange house, troubled, and chilled to the very heart.

From time to time she went over to examine her ailing chickens, removing a dead bird from the nest to give a chance of life to the others. And each time it seemed that there was a silent lament in the wind blowing through broken panes in the attic, like the mysterious grief of children unknown.

'It used to be Frantz's house,' said my companion at last, 'when he was small. He had wanted a house of his very own, away from everyone, where he could go whenever he liked, to play, and even to live. My father was so amused at such a strange fancy that he couldn't refuse. So on Thursdays and Sundays, or whenever he felt in the mood, Frantz would go off to stay in his own house like a grown-up. Children from the farms round about would come here to play with him and help him keep house, or work in the garden. It was a marvellous game. When night came he was never afraid of sleeping here alone. As for us, we admired him so much, it never occurred to us to be uneasy about him.

'But for a long time now the house has been empty. My father is too old and care-worn to go looking for my brother or appeal to him to come home. For that matter what could he have done?

'I often come here. The country children come and play in the yard as before. I like to think of them as Frantz's former playmates, and of him as still a child who will come back one day with the girl he chose for his wife.

'The children all know me. I play with them. These chickens were ours . . .'

This pathetic little tragedy of the storm had brought her to confide to me the deep grief of which she had never spoken, her sorrow for the loss of a brother so endearing and so loved, whatever his follies . . . And I listened in silence, my heart swollen with tears unshed.

The doors and the gate locked up once more, the chickens restored to their wooden coop behind the house, she took my arm in sadness and I led her home.

Weeks went by, then months. I am speaking of a far-away time – a vanished happiness. It fell to me to befriend, to console with whatever words I could find, one who had been the fairy, the princess, the mysterious love-dream of our adolescence – and it fell to me because my companion had fled. Of that period, of the conversations in the evenings after a day of teaching on the little hill at Saint-Benoist-des-Champs, of our long walks when the one subject that filled our minds was the subject we had decided never to mention, what can I say? I've kept a single image of that time, and it is already fading: the image of a lovely face grown thin and of two eyes whose lids slowly droop as they glance at me, as if her gaze was unable to dwell on anything but an inner world.

And I remained her faithful companion – sharing with her the long wait which we never spoke of – during the whole of a spring and summer unlike any there will ever be again. Several times, in the afternoons, we went back to Frantz's house. She would open the doors and windows, for there must be no sign of damp or mould when the young couple came home. She saw to the needs of the half-wild fowls in the yard behind the house, and on school holidays we helped to organize games among the children from the farms whose laughing voices in this isolated setting made the little house seem even more empty and forlorn.

A CONVERSATION IN THE RAIN

AUGUST, and the close of the summer term, took me away
from the neighbourhood of Les Sablonnières and Yvonne de
Galais, for I was to spend the two-month holiday at Sainte-
Agathe. So again I saw the big bare courtyard and the empty
school-room where everything reminded me of *le grand
Meaulnes*. Each corner held some souvenir of our adolescence,
now at an end. I spent a great part of the long yellow days
shut up in a corner of the Public Records office as in the time
before he came to us, or in one of the class-rooms. I read, or
wrote, or dreamed . . . My father was away fishing; Millie was
in the sitting-room sewing or playing the piano as in the old
days. And in the stillness of the class-room the torn sheets of
green foolscap, the discarded wrappings of book prizes, the
sponged blackboard – all announced that the year was finished,
the rewards distributed, and everything at a standstill till
October when a new effort would have to be made – and I
thought: our youth is finished too, and we've failed to find
happiness. I, too, could only wait for the new term, and Les
Sablonnières, and the return of Augustin who might never
return . . .

There was, however, one piece of good news I could im-
part to Millie when she got round to pumping me about the
young bride. I was dreading her questions, for she had a way
at once innocent and shrewd of taking you off guard by putting
a finger on your most hidden thought. So I cut the ground
from under her by saying straight off that my friend's wife was
expecting a baby in October.

Privately I was thinking of the day when Yvonne de Galais
made this important piece of news known to me. For a moment I had been tongue-tied, with the embarrassment of a
very young man. Then, to cover the fact that I was embarrassed, and without stopping to think what unhealed wounds
I might reopen, I had blurted out:

'You must be very happy.'

But smiling serenely, with no hint of irony, rancour, or regret, she had replied:

'Yes, very happy.'

During this last week of the holidays which is in some ways the best of all and the most romantic – a week of pelting rain and blazing fires, a week I usually devoted to shooting in the damp black woods around Vieux-Nançay – I made plans to return directly to Saint-Benoist-des-Champs, because Firmin, Aunt Julie, and the girls at Vieux-Nançay would have asked too many awkward questions. So for once I renounced the excitement of living the life of a country sportsman for a week and went straight to my school-house, arriving there one afternoon four days before the beginning of classes.

Already the yard was carpeted with yellow leaves. When the carrier had left I went into the echoing musty dining-room and drearily unpacked the hamper Millie had provided me with. After a hasty meal, nervous and restless, I put on my cape and set out feverishly on a long walk that took me to Les Sablonnières.

I hesitated to present myself without warning on the very first evening of my return, but bolder now than in February, after taking a turn round the house, where the only light to be seen was at her window, I went round to the back and got over a fence into the garden, where I sat on a bench near the hedge in the gathering dusk, happy just to be there, so close to the source of all that absorbed my thoughts and troubled my heart.

It was growing dark and a thin rain had commenced to fall. I stared at my boots, vaguely aware that they were growing wet and glistening. The darkness and the chill of evening slowly encroached on my reveries without disturbing them. Yearningly I thought of the muddy lanes at Sainte-Agathe on this September evening; I saw the misty Square, the butcher's boy whistling as he went to fetch water at the pump, the café with its bright lights, and a cheerful carriage-load of people with open umbrellas arriving at Uncle Florentin's towards the end of the holidays . . . And I was thinking: what an empty

178

happiness when Meaulnes, my companion, cannot be there to share it, nor his young wife . . .

When, looking up, I saw her within a few paces. Her shoes on the gravel made a sound I had confused with the dripping of water from the hedge. She had thrown a long black woollen shawl over her head and shoulders, and the rain had laid a silvery powder over her hair. She must have seen me from her window overlooking the garden. And she was walking towards me. It reminded me of Millie, in days gone by, coming out to fetch me in and then, finding it not at all unpleasant to wander about in the dark and the rain, saying gently, 'You'll catch your death,' and staying out with me for a good long talk . . .

Yvonne de Galais held out her hand, which was burning hot, and, giving up the idea of asking me into the house, sat down on the mossy green-stained bench, one side of which was fairly dry, while I stood, one knee resting on the bench, leaning forward to listen.

She began by reproaching me in a friendly way for having cut short my holidays.

'I felt I should come back as soon as ever I could, to keep you company.'

'You're right,' she murmured with a sigh. 'I'm still alone. Augustin hasn't come back . . .'

Interpreting her sigh as a confession of sorrow, even of reluctant reproach, I ventured:

'To think that anyone so truly noble could be so foolish! . . . Perhaps, stronger than anything else, the taste for adventure . . .'

But she interrupted me. And it was there, in the garden, on that wet evening, that for the first and last time she talked to me about Meaulnes.

'You mustn't speak like that, François Seurel, my friend,' she gently admonished. 'For it is we – it is I who am the guilty one. Think what we did . . .

'We said to him: here is your happiness, here is what you spent your whole youth looking for, here is the girl you saw in all your dreams!

'How could anyone, pushed by the shoulders like that,

179

avoid a reaction of indecision, then fear, then dismay – how could he resist the temptation to escape?'

'But Yvonne,' I gently reminded her, 'you knew that *you* were that happiness! That girl was *you*!'

'Ah!' she sighed. 'How could I for one moment have had such a conceited idea! That was the cause of it all.

'I once said to you: "Perhaps I can't do anything for him." But in my heart I was thinking: "Because he has looked for me so long, and because I love him, I simply must make him happy." And then, when I saw him beside me, feverish, restless, consumed with some mysterious remorse, I knew I was as powerless as any other woman . . .

'"I'm not worthy of you," he kept saying, when it was dawn, after our wedding night.

'And I did what I could to solace and reassure him. But nothing could relieve his distress.

'At last I said:

'"If you feel you ought to go, if I came to you at a moment when nothing could make you happy, if it's necessary for you to leave me now for a time and only come back when you've found peace, then it is I who ask you to go" . . .'

In the darkness I could see that she had raised her eyes and was looking at me. It was as though she had made a confession and was waiting, anxiously, for me either to approve or condemn. But what could I say? I had of course my own picture of *le grand Meaulnes* from the days when, rigid and untamed, he would accept punishment rather than apologize or ask a favour which would certainly have been granted. I felt that Yvonne de Galais should have been more drastic with him, that she should have taken his head between her hands and said: 'It doesn't matter what you may have done; no man is blameless; and I love you . . .' I felt she had made a great mistake out of generosity, in a spirit of self-sacrifice, to put him back on the path of adventure . . . But how could I find fault with so much goodness, so much love?

There was a long silence. Too deeply moved to speak, we listened to the cold rain dripping from the hedge and from the branches of the trees.

'And so,' she concluded, 'he left that morning. We had reached an understanding, and he kissed me like a husband parting from his young wife to go on a long voyage ...'

She rose, and I took her feverish hand, then her arm, and we walked along the path in the darkness which was now complete.

'And yet,' I said, 'he hasn't written to you once.'

'No,' she replied. 'Not once.'

And then, as we were both thinking of the hazardous life he might be leading on the roads of France or Germany, we began to speak of him as we had never done before. Forgotten details, old impressions came to mind as we went slowly towards the house, stopping every few steps to remind one another of things he had said or done. For a long while, in the dark, making our way slowly through the garden, I listened to her low clear voice; and for my part, caught up again in my old enthusiasm, I talked long and freely, with deep affection, of the friend who had deserted us ...

12

THE BURDEN

SCHOOL was to open on Monday. On Saturday afternoon, at about five, a woman from the domain came into the yard where I was sawing wood for the winter. She told me that a little girl had been born at Les Sablonnières. It had been a difficult confinement. At nine in the evening they had sent for the midwife at Préveranges. At midnight someone had driven to Vierzon for a doctor. He had been obliged to use forceps. The baby's head was injured and she cried a good deal but seemed otherwise all that could be desired. Yvonne de Galais was now extremely weak, but had endured her ordeal with extraordinary courage.

I put down my saw, hurried indoors to get an overcoat, and, pleased on the whole with the news, accompanied the peasant woman to Les Sablonnières. Cautiously, for fear one or the other of the patients might be sleeping, I mounted the wooden staircase to the first floor. And there Monsieur de Galais, tired but smiling, showed me into a room where for the time being a curtained cradle had been installed.

It was the first time I had entered a house on the day a baby had been born there. How bizarre and mysterious it seemed to me, and how good! It was such a fine evening, almost like summer, that Monsieur de Galais had ventured to open the window overlooking the yard. Leaning against the window-sill, worn out by his vigil but happy, he related the dramatic events of the previous night, and as I listened I was vaguely conscious of a strange presence in the room with us . . .

Behind the curtain 'it' set up a thin little wail. Then in a whisper Monsieur de Galais said:

'It's the injury on the head that makes her cry.'

Mechanically – one felt that he had been doing it since morning and had got into the way of it – he began to rock the little bundle of curtains.

'She's laughed already, and she holds on to your finger. Oh, but you haven't seen her!'

He parted the curtains and I saw a tiny red swollen face and a narrow little head that seemed slightly deformed.

'It's nothing,' Monsieur de Galais assured me. 'The doctor says it will come right of itself . . . Give her your finger, she'll hang on to it.'

I discovered a world quite unknown to me, and my heart was swelling with a new kind of joy . . .

Monsieur de Galais cautiously opened the door to the next room.

'She's not asleep. Would you like to go in?'

Her face was hectic as she lay there with her fair hair spread over the pillow. She held out her hand and smiled wearily. I complimented her on her daughter. In a slightly hoarse voice, and with unusual harshness – the harshness of someone emerging from combat – she said:

'Yes, but they damaged her!' The accusation was, however, softened by her smile.

We left soon afterwards for fear of tiring her.

The next afternoon, Sunday, I was hurrying over towards Les Sablonnières in an almost cheerful mood. At the door my hand was already lifted when I saw a notice pinned up:

Please do not ring

It didn't occur to me that anything was amiss. I knocked instead, quite loudly. I heard someone coming quickly, but with muffled tread. A stranger opened the door. It was the doctor from Vierzon.

Only then did I feel any alarm. 'Is anything wrong?' I asked sharply.

'Sh . . . sh . . .' He seemed angry and spoke in whispers. He told me that the baby had nearly died during the night, that the mother was extremely ill . . .

In great dismay I followed him on tiptoe up the stairs. The baby, asleep in her cradle, was now quite pale – as white as a little corpse. The doctor seemed to think he could save her. As for the mother, he would not commit himself, but went into long explanations, as if I were the one friend of the family . . . He spoke of congestion of the lungs, of embolism; he hesitated, seemed uncertain . . .

Then Monsieur de Galais came in. He was pale and shaky and had aged shockingly in the last two days. With a vague sort of gesture he led me into her room.

'Be careful not to alarm her,' he whispered. 'The doctor says she must be made to feel everything is going well.'

Lying there with flaming cheeks, her head thrown back, her eyes now and then rolling as if she were strangling, Yvonne de Galais was fighting against death patiently and with heart-breaking valour.

She was unable to speak but held out her hand with such friendliness that I could scarcely keep from breaking down.

'Well now!' Monsieur de Galais was saying loudly, with a ghastly and almost insane good cheer, 'for a sick woman she doesn't look too bad, does she?'

I couldn't reply; I could only keep hold of the hand that was burning into me, the hand of someone dying . . .

She made an effort to say something, to ask me something,

heaven knows what. She turned her eyes first towards me, then towards the window, as if she wished me to go out and look for someone . . . But she was seized by an acute attack of suffocation; the beautiful blue eyes which a moment before had been making some tragic appeal turned back with only the whites showing; her cheeks and brow turned dark, and she fought on patiently, pressing back to the very end any sign of terror or despair. People came running – the doctors, the women – a jar of oxygen was produced, and towels and bottles – and all the while the old man bent over the bed fairly shouting – as if she were already far away – in a harsh and trembling voice:

'Don't be afraid, Yvonne. It's nothing. You've nothing to be afraid of.'

The crisis passed, and she was able to get a few breaths. But the attacks persisted, as with eyes rolling she struggled on, unable even for an instant to escape from the abyss into which she had already sunk to give me a glance, or a word.

. . . As I could do nothing to help, I made up my mind to leave. I might, of course, have stayed a few moments longer, and now when I think of it I am tormented with regret. But at the moment I was still hopeful. I felt that the end could not possibly be so near.

Once outside, I walked to the edge of the fir wood behind the house, haunted by the look Yvonne had turned towards the window. Like a sentinel, or a detective tracking down a fugitive, I scanned the depths of this wood through which Augustin had first come to the domain and through which he had gone away last winter. But there was absolutely no sign of life – no dubious shadow, not even a moving branch. Until, some time later, from the direction of the Préveranges road, I heard the tinkling sound of a bell. And before long, at a turning in the path, I saw a boy in a smock wearing the red cap of an acolyte. He was followed by a priest . . . I turned away, swallowing my tears.

Next day school was due to open. At seven, two or three boys were already in the yard. I waited as long as possible before going down and showing myself. And when at last I was turning the key of the musty class-room which had been shut up for two months, what I had been dreading more than anything in the world came to pass: the oldest boy turned away from a group playing under the shelter and walked towards me. He came to tell me that 'the young lady of Les Sablonnières' had died in the early hours of the evening.

Everything around me is confused and merged into pain. I feel I shall never have strength enough to resume my work. Even to cross the bare playground calls for an effort which will break my knees. All is pain and bitterness, because she is dead. The world is empty, the holidays are ended – ended, too, the long country drives, and the mysterious fête . . . all is sorrow again, as it was before . . .

I tell the children they are free for the day. They slip away to tell the news to the other boys and all the countryside. I get out a braided coat I possess, take down my black hat, and walk miserably away towards Les Sablonnières . . .

. . . Here I am, in front of the house which three years ago we all but gave up hope of finding. And it is in this house that Yvonne de Galais, the wife of Augustin Meaulnes, died last night. Enshrouded since yesterday in silence, isolated in its own desolation, it might be mistaken for a chapel.

So this is what the bright morning of a new term had in store for us, this perfidious autumn sun filtering through the branches. How am I to fight back bitter revolt and tears that choke me! We had at last found the beautiful girl, and we had won her. She was the wife of my companion and I loved her with the deep and secret devotion for which there can be no words. I looked at her and was content, like a child. One day I too might have wished to marry, and she would have been the first to whom I would have confided the secret . . .

The notice is still pinned to the door, close to the bell. The coffin is already there in the vestibule. Upstairs it is the baby's nurse who receives me, and tells me about the last moments, then quietly opens the door . . . And I see her. The fever has gone and the hectic flush; the struggle is over, and the long waiting. Nothing remains but stillness and a white face surrounded by cotton-wool, a face inflexible and unfeeling, and a dead brow framed in thick and lifeless hair.

Monsieur de Galais, in stocking-feet, his back to us, crouches in a corner pawing with a fearful tenacity over the contents of drawers pulled out from a chest. Now and then he comes upon an old photograph of his daughter, already faded, and as he looks at it begins to sob, his shoulders shaking as if with uncontrollable laughter.

She is to be buried at noon. The doctor is afraid of the rapid decomposition that sometimes occurs in cases of embolism. That explains why her face and body are packed in cotton-wool saturated with phenol.

When they have dressed her – in her fine gown of dark blue velvet spangled with small silver stars whose leg-of-mutton sleeves, no longer in fashion, have to be flattened and creased – it is time to bring up the coffin. It proves to be too long for the turn in the narrow staircase. Someone proposes hoisting it to the window by means of a rope and lowering it in the same way. But Monsieur de Galais, still bent over a heap of old objects in his search for heaven knows what lost memories, breaks in with a terrible vehemence, and in a voice choked with angry tears he protests:

'No! Rather than allow anything so horrible, I'll carry her in my own arms . . .'

And he would have done so, at the risk of succumbing under the weight and crashing downstairs with her.

Then I step forward. There is only one thing to be done: with the aid of the doctor and one of the women I pass one arm under the back of the outstretched body, the other under the knees, and lift her up. My left arm supporting her, her shoulder against my right arm, her head fallen forward under my chin, she weighs terribly on my heart. I descend the long steep stairway very slowly, step by step, while down below everything is being made ready.

Soon both arms are aching. At each step, with this burden on my breast, I find it more difficult to breathe. Holding close the inert, heavy body, I bend over her head and take a deep breath, drawing into my mouth some strands of golden hair:

dead hair that has a taste of earth. This taste of earth and of death, and this weight on my heart, is all that is left to me of the great adventure, and of you, Yvonne de Galais, so ardently sought, so deeply loved . . .

13

THE EXERCISE-BOOK

In the house peopled with sad mementoes, where all day long women were rocking and comforting a small ailing baby, it was not long before Monsieur de Galais took to his bed. With the first cold spell of winter the spark of life went quietly out and I found myself shedding tears at the bedside of this charming old man whose indulgence, and the fanciful mind he shared with his son, had been the cause of our whole adventure. Fortunately he died in complete ignorance of all that had happened and, indeed, in an almost total silence. Having been for years without relatives or friends in this part of France, he had named me his residuary legatee until the return of Meaulnes, to whom I was to render full account, if ever he did return . . . And from that time I lived at Les Sablonnières, though retaining my post as teacher at Saint-Benoist. Each morning I set out in the early hours for the village, taking with me a lunch that could be warmed up on the school-room stove. And as soon as the afternoon study period was finished I came home. This arrangement made it possible for me to have the baby with me – she was looked after by the women of the farm – it also increased my chances of meeting Augustin in case he should ever find his way back.

Besides, I was always hoping that somewhere in the house, in a closet, perhaps, in a drawer, I might come upon some paper or some object that would throw light on the manner in which his life had been spent during the long silence of the preceding years – some clue which would explain the reasons for his flight or at least suggest a direction in which to look for him . . . I had already gone through I don't know how many cupboards and wardrobes, and examined stacks of cartons filled with packets of letters and old family photographs, or with artificial flowers, feathers, aigrettes, and birds long since out of style. The faded scents, reminders of so much that was dead and gone, aroused in my own mind memories which for a whole day filled me with depression and brought the search to an end . . .

And then one day, a holiday, up in the attic, I noticed a small trunk, long and flat, covered in rough pig-skin with the hairs half worn away, and recognized it as the box Augustin had brought with him to Sainte-Agathe. How stupid, I thought, not to have looked here in the first place! I had no trouble in forcing the rusty lock, and found the trunk crammed with old textbooks – grammar, arithmetic, literature – and exercise-books of every description . . . Prompted more by sentiment than curiosity I rummaged among them, re-reading dictated passages I knew by heart, so often had we recopied them: Rousseau's 'Aqueduct' – 'An Adventure in Calabria' by P.-L. Courier – 'Letter from George Sand to her Son' . . .

There was also a 'Composition Test Book' and this surprised me, because these test books were school property and never taken away. On its green cover, faded at the edges, the name of the student, Augustin Meaulnes, was printed in a bold round-hand. From the date on the first page, April 189 . ., I knew that he had commenced it only a few days before leaving Sainte-Agathe. The first pages had been written with the religious application we were expected to show in this particular branch of our work – the following pages were blank, and that was no doubt why he had kept the book.

Kneeling on the floor, reminded of all the petty rules and regulations that had assumed such importance in our adolescent routine, I was thumbing the pages when I found there was writing on some of the other pages. After four blank leaves, another series of entries began.

It was the same handwriting, but less painstaking, indeed at times a rapid scribble which was scarcely legible: short paragraphs separated by a skipped line or two. Sometimes merely half a sentence. Here and there a date. From the first line I guessed that these pages would reveal something of his life in Paris, possibly afford a clue to his present whereabouts, and I went downstairs to read the document at leisure, by a better light than was available in the dim attic. It was a bright winter day, sunny but uncertain. At moments the sun projected in sharp outline against the white curtain the crossed pattern of the sashes, then a gust of wind would fling a brief shower against the panes. It was by this window, near the fire, that I read the lines which explained so much and which I reproduce word for word . . .

14

THE SECRET

I WALKED past her window again. The double curtains are still drawn, showing up white against the dusty panes. Even were Yvonne de Galais to open it, what could I say to her now that she is married? What is there left for me? How am I to go on?

Saturday, 13 February. On the quay I met the girl who, like me, had been waiting in front of the closed house last June and who told me about it. I spoke to her. As we walked, I glanced at her and noticed the slight flaws in her appearance: a faint line at the corner of her mouth, cheeks a little too hollow, a trace of powder showing near her nose. Suddenly she turned and looked straight at me, perhaps because she is prettier full-face than in profile. Then she said in a dry sort of way: 'You amuse me. You remind me of a boy who once courted me, in Bourges. We were even engaged . . .'

It is night already and there is no one about. The gas street lamp is reflected on the wet pavement. Suddenly she moves nearer and asks me to take her and her sister to a theatre, tonight. For the first time I notice she is in mourning. She wears a hat too old for her youthful face and carries a long umbrella as thin as a walking-stick. I am standing close to her and when I make a gesture my finger-nails catch in the crêpe of her bodice. I offer some pretext for not granting the request. Offended, she turns to go. And now I'm the one who does the approaching and the asking. A workman going by in the darkness whispers banteringly: 'Don't you go with him, my dear; you might get hurt.' And we stand there, embarrassed, both of us.

At the theatre. The two girls, my friend whose name is Valentine Blondeau and her sister, arrive wearing cheap scarves.

Valentine sits in front of me. Every little while she turns uneasily, as if trying to make me out. All I know is that to be near her makes me feel almost happy, and each time I respond with a smile.

The women around us wore very low-necked dresses. We made jokes about them. At first she smiled, then she said: 'Who am I to laugh! My own dress is too low.' And she drew her scarf up round her shoulders. Indeed under its square of black lace I could see that in her hurry to change her dress she had turned down the top of her plain linen chemise.

There is something about her that suggests both poverty and *naïveté* and in her eyes something both pathetic and venturesome that attracts me. When I'm with her – the only person who has ever been able to tell me anything about the people at the domain – I am continuously reminded of that strange old adventure. I wanted to find out more about the little house on the boulevard, but she met my questions with such embarrassing ones of her own that I couldn't even reply. I feel that from now on we shall both avoid that subject. And yet I also know I shall see her again. But why? What good can come of it? Can it be that I'm condemned to tag along after anyone who can evoke, if only in the vaguest and most fleeting way, an echo of the adventure I failed in . . .

At midnight alone in the empty street, I ask myself the meaning of this new and somewhat capricious episode. I walk past rows of houses like so many cardboard boxes piled one on top of the other in which a whole population is asleep. And I suddenly remember a decision I had taken a month ago: I had resolved to go there some night, around one in the morning, find my way to the back of the house, get into the garden, enter like a thief, and search the place for some clue that would lead me to the lost domain, to see her once more, only to see her ... But I'm tired and hungry. I too made haste to change for the theatre and went without dinner. Restless, nervous, I sit on the edge of my bed a long while before putting out the light, and my conscience bothers me. But why?

A fact worth noting: they wouldn't let me see them to their door, or even tell me where they live. But I followed them as long as I could. I know they live in a little street not far from Notre-Dame. The number I don't know. I think they must be dressmakers or milliners.

Unknown to her sister, Valentine gave me a rendezvous for tomorrow, Thursday, at four, in front of the same theatre. 'If I'm not there,' she said, 'come back on Friday at the same time, and Saturday, and so on ...'

Thursday, 18 February. I set out to keep the appointment in a strong wind heavy with stored-up rain. I kept thinking, 'It's bound to pour in the end.'

I walk through the dim streets feeling depressed. A drop of rain falls. I dread the prospect of rain: a heavy shower might prevent her from coming. But the wind strengthens and blows it all somewhere else. Up there in the grey afternoon sky – now grey, now dazzling – a great cloud has had to surrender to the wind. And I'm down here, glued to the earth, wretchedly waiting ...

Outside the theatre. After fifteen minutes I know she won't be coming. From the quay I look away towards the bridge she would have had to cross and watch the endless procession. My eyes pick out every young woman in mourning, and I feel a kind of gratitude towards the ones who for the longest time, till they are quite near, have looked enough like her to keep my hope alive . . .

An hour of waiting. I am weary. In the twilight a policeman goes by. He is conducting to the nearest police station a miscreant who mutters all the insults and obscenities he can think of. The officer is furious, white-faced but silent. As they reach the corridor he begins to strike. Then he closes the door and is free to beat the poor devil at leisure . . . A horrible fancy takes hold of me: I have renounced heaven and stand impatiently at the gates of hell.

Losing heart at last, I give up and walk off to the narrow street between the cathedral and the Seine. I know approximately the location of the building they live in, and for a while I pace up and down. Occasionally a maid or a housewife comes out into the drizzle to make a few purchases before nightfall . . . There is no point in my staying here, so I leave . . . I turn back to the Square where we were to have met. The bright rain seems to retard the coming of darkness. There are more people about now than an hour ago, a black swarm . . .

Suppositions – despair – fatigue – I cling to the thought: tomorrow. Tomorrow, at the same time, at the same place, I will be waiting for her. And I am impatient for tomorrow to arrive. I look forward with boredom to the evening that lies before me, and the long empty morning . . . But at least this day is all but finished . . . Back in my room, before the fire, I can hear news-vendors hawking the evening papers. No doubt in some attic room hidden away behind Notre-Dame she hears them too.

She . . . I mean: Valentine.

The evening, which I had wanted to conjure away, weighs on me strangely. As the hour advances, as the day draws to a close while I long for it to end, there are men who have invested in it all their hopes, all their love, the last ounce of their strength. There are men at the point of death, and men facing an overdue note, who are praying that tomorrow may never come. Others know they will wake up with a feeling of guilt.

Some are so tired that this night will never be long enough to give them all the rest they need. And by what right do I, who have wasted this day, make claims on tomorrow?

Friday evening. I had been expecting to write here: 'I have not seen her again.' And that would have ended it.

But when I arrived at the theatre at four this afternoon, there she was. Slim and sedate, dressed in black but with powder on her face, and at her throat a white collar that gave her the look of a guilty pierrot, half pathetic half guileful.

She came only to tell me that she must leave at once, that this is the last time...

For all that, as day turns into night, we are still together, slowly walking side by side over the gravelled paths of the Tuileries. She has been telling me about herself, but in such a roundabout way I'm not much the wiser. She says 'my lover' when referring to the fiancé she failed to marry. She does it on purpose, I think, to shock me and put me off.

Here are some remarks of hers which I set down almost against my will:

'Don't trust me, because all I've ever done is make silly mistakes.'

'I've roamed all over the place, all alone.'

'I drove my fiancé to despair. I left him because he admired me too much. He only saw me the way he imagined me, not as I really am. And the fact is, I'm full of faults. We would only have been wretched.'

I keep catching her trying to make herself out worse than she is. I think she is trying to convince herself that she was right in behaving so foolishly, that she has nothing to regret, that she was unworthy of the good fortune held out to her.

Once she said, looking at me steadily:

'What I like about you, and I've no idea why, is my memories...'

Again:

'I still love him, more than you think.'

Then suddenly, sharply, crudely, unhappily:

'After all, just what is it you want? Are you in love with me too? Do you, too, want to marry me?'

I stammered out something, I don't know what. Perhaps I said: 'Yes.'

The fragmentary diary broke off there. It was followed by rough draughts of letters – illegible, formless, with phrases scratched out.

Their engagement must have been a precarious one. At Meaulnes's request the girl gave up her work. It was he who made all the preparations for the wedding. But continuously harassed by the need to resume his search, to explore any new trail that might lead to his lost love, he seems to have vanished from time to time, for there were letters in which, with a tragic embarrassment, he sought to justify himself in Valentine's eyes.

15

THE SECRET

CONTINUED

THEN the diary was resumed.

There were notes referring to a trip they had taken into the country – I don't know where. But for some reason, from this point on, possibly due to an instinctive reserve about purely private matters, the entries were so fragmentary and formless, often a mere scrawl, that I've been obliged to re-edit all this part of his story.

14 June. When he woke up in his room at the inn, the sun was already up and its beams made vivid the red designs on the black curtains. Farm labourers in the café below were talking loudly as they drank their morning coffee; indignant but stolid, they were passing harsh judgements on one of their employers. For some time no doubt Meaulnes had been hear-

ing in his sleep this peaceful din, for at first he paid no attention. The curtain spattered with clusters of grapes made red by the sun, the morning voices finding their way into the silent room – it all blended into the single impression of waking up in the heart of the country on the first day of a long and blissful vacation.

He got out of bed, crossed the room, and knocked gently at the door of the adjoining room. Getting no reply, he opened it without a sound. Then he saw Valentine and was at once aware of the source of his peaceful contentment. She was asleep, so still and silent that she seemed not to be breathing. He thought: that's how birds must sleep. For some time he stood looking at her sleeping, childlike face, so perfectly tranquil that it seemed a pity it should ever be disturbed.

The only movement she made to show that she was no longer sleeping was to raise her eyelids and look at him.

As soon as she was dressed Meaulnes went back to her room. 'We're late,' she said.

And, like a housewife in her own home, she at once proceeded to tidy the rooms and brush the clothes Meaulnes had been wearing the night before. When she came to the trousers she heaved a sigh, for they were thickly spattered with mud. She hesitated, examined the spots, then carefully scraped away the mud with a knife before taking up the brush again.

'That's what the boys at Sainte-Agathe used to do,' said Meaulnes, 'when they'd fallen into the mud.'

'It's how my mother used to do it,' said Valentine.

. . . And it was just such a companion that would have suited *le grand Meaulnes* peasant and hunter, before his mysterious adventure . . .

15 June. At the farm, where thanks to some acquaintances who had introduced them as man and wife, they were invited to dinner – much to their annoyance – she had shown all the timidity of a young bride.

At each end of the table covered in white linen, candlesticks had been placed, as if for a quiet country wedding celebration.

Faces round the table, as they leaned forward in this dim light, were at once plunged in shadow.

Valentine sat on the right of Patrice, the farmer's son, and Meaulnes was beside her. All through the meal he was taciturn, although most of the remarks were addressed to him. Ever since his decision, for the sake of appearances, to treat Valentine as his wife in this out-of-the-way village, he had felt uncomfortable and guilty. And while Patrice, in the manner of a country squire, did the honours, Meaulnes was thinking:

'It's I who should be presiding at my own marriage feast tonight, in a big room with a low ceiling like this one, a beautiful room I can still see . . .'

By his side Valentine timidly refused everything that was offered her. Like a young peasant woman. The more they plied her, the more she seemed to turn to her friend for protection. For some time Patrice had been vainly urging her to empty her glass. At last Meaulnes bent over her and said gently:

'My dear Valentine, you must drink something.'

With a docile air she lifted the glass to her lips. Patrice smiled and congratulated him on having such an obedient wife.

But the two guests remained silent and thoughtful. For one thing they were tired; their shoes were wet and muddy from the long walk, and the newly washed tiles of the kitchen floor were cold under their feet. Moreover, from time to time the young man was forced to say:

'My wife . . . Valentine, my wife . . .'

And each time he murmured the word, in the hearing of these alien peasants, in this alien room, he felt he was doing something wrong.

17 June. The afternoon of this last day began badly.

Patrice and his wife went for a walk with them. Gradually, on the rough hill-side covered in heather, the two couples got farther apart. Meaulnes and Valentine sat down in a little patch of underbrush between clumps of juniper.

The sky was low and the wind brought an occasional sprinkle. The evening seemed to have a bitter taste, the taste of a weariness that not even love could dispel.

For some time they stayed in their shelter under the branches, exchanging only a few words. Then the skies lifted. And the sudden improvement in the weather brought them out of their moodiness.

They began to speak of love, or rather it was Valentine who talked, and talked . . .

'I must tell you,' she said, 'what my fiancé promised me – he was such a child, really. We were to have our own house immediately, a sort of cottage hidden away in the country. He said it was all ready for us. It would be like arriving home after a long absence, the evening of our wedding – about this time of day, just before dark. And in the lanes and the court, from the shrubbery, unknown children would be there to greet us and cry out: "Long live the bride!" You can see how fantastic he was . . .'

As he listened to her, arrested, disturbed, Meaulnes seemed to be hearing the echo of a voice he knew. He was also aware of something in her tone as she told her story that was close to regret.

From his manner she was afraid she had hurt him, and turned to him impulsively, trustingly:

'I'm going to give you all I have to give: something which till now has been my most precious possession . . . and I want you to burn it.'

Watching him closely, apprehensively, she took from her pocket a little packet of letters – the letters her fiancé had written her, and handed it to him.

In a flash he had recognized the fine handwriting. In a flash he accused himself of not having guessed the identity of her fiancé at once. Before his eyes was the writing of Frantz the vagabond, the same writing he had seen on the despairing note left behind in a room of the château . . .

They were now walking along a narrow path through a field where daisies grew in the grass made bright by the slanting rays of the late afternoon sun. Meaulnes was in such a state of disarray that he hadn't begun to think of what bearing this revelation might have on his own situation. He read because she had asked him to read. Childish phrases

197

– sentimental, touching . . . This one, for example, in the last letter:

So you lost the little heart, unforgivable little Valentine. What will happen to us now? A good thing I'm not superstitious . . .

Meaulnes read on, half blind with rage and sorrow, his face set, but pale, with a twitching under his eyes. Alarmed, Valentine glanced at the page before him, to see how far he had got, to see what could have made him so angry . . .

Then she hastily explained. 'Oh, the heart! It was a trinket he'd given me, making me swear to keep it always. Just one of his crazy ideas.'

But she merely succeeded in exasperating Meaulnes.

'Crazy!' he exclaimed, thrusting the letters in his pocket. 'Why do you keep on saying "crazy"? Why couldn't you have taken him at his word? I knew him. He was the most wonderful chap that ever lived!'

'You knew him!' she exclaimed, as if unable to believe her ears. 'You knew Frantz de Galais!'

'He was my best friend, we were fellow adventurers, we were like brothers – and now I've stolen his fiancée!

'Ah!' he went on, with mounting anger, 'if you knew the harm you've done! By refusing to believe! It's all your doing. It's through you that everything is lost, everything . . .'

Overwhelmed, she tried to speak, to take his hand, but he thrust her roughly aside.

'Go away. Leave me alone.'

'Very well,' she said, her voice unsteady, her cheeks flaming, her eyes filling with tears. 'If that's the way it is, I'll go – certainly. I'll go back to Bourges with my sister. And if you don't come for me, you know, of course, that my father is too poor to keep me at home. So the only thing for me in that case will be to go back to Paris. I'll take to the road as I did once before, and now that I've lost my only means of earning a living, you know what will become of me . . .'

She went off to pack her belongings and take them to the station. Meaulnes, without even a glance at her retreating figure, kept walking on wherever his feet might carry him.

Again there was a break in the diary.

Then came more rough drafts of the letters of a man unable to make up his mind, a man adrift. From La Ferté-d'Angillon he wrote, ostensibly to confirm his decision never to see her again and explain why in detail, but perhaps in the secret hope of receiving an answer. In one letter he asked her a question about the domain which, in his disarray, had not even occurred to him at the time: did she know where it was? . . .

In another he implored her to make up her quarrel with Frantz de Galais. He himself would undertake to find him . . . Some of the letters had probably never been sent, but he must have posted two or three without getting a reply. It had been a period of inner conflict, of misery and utter loneliness. When there was no further hope of seeing Yvonne de Galais again, he must have felt his resolution weaken. And from the following pages – the last in the diary – I gather that he hired a bicycle one morning at the beginning of the holidays and rode over to Bourges, 'to visit the cathedral'.

He set out first thing in the morning, taking the fine straight road through the forest, and must have invented on the way a hundred pretexts for presenting himself before the woman he had cast off without loss of face, and without asking for a reconciliation.

The last few pages, which I have put into some sort of order, tell of this trip and this final mistake . . .

16

THE SECRET

CONCLUSION

25 AUGUST. On the far side of Bourges, at the end of the last suburb, and after a lengthy search, he found the house. A woman – Valentine Blondeau's mother – seemed to be waiting for him on the doorstep. She was a respectable-looking housewife, a little heavy, rather shabby, but still personable. She

watched him approach with some curiosity, and when he asked if Mademoiselle Blondeau were at home, she replied politely, in a friendly tone, that they had left for Paris ten days before.

'They made me promise not to say where they were going,' she added, 'but any letters sent to their former address would be forwarded.'

As he turned away and pushed his bicycle down the path he was thinking:

'She's gone . . . It's ended the way I meant it to end . . . It's I who forced her into it. ''You know what will become of me,'' she said. And I'm the one who brought her to that. It's I who have sent Frantz's fiancée on to the streets.'

Under his breath he muttered: 'So much the better! So much the better!' Knowing well that it was so much the worse and fearing that, with this woman's eyes on him, he would stumble and fall to his knees before reaching the gate.

He had no mind for lunch but sat down in a café to write a long letter to Valentine, if only to give voice to the despairing cries that pushed up for a hearing till he was nearly choked by them. The letter repeated over and over: 'How could you! . . . How could you! . . . How could you stoop to that! . . . How could you throw yourself into the gutter . . .'

At a near-by table some officers were drinking. One of them was recounting an amorous exploit in a loud voice: '. . . so I said to her, ''but you *must* know me, I play cards with your husband every evening!''' The others laughed, and turned to spit behind the bench. Gaunt and dust-stained, Meaulnes stared at them as a beggar might have done. He pictured Valentine with them, sitting on their knees.

For some time he rode round the cathedral, telling himself glumly: 'After all, it's what I came to see.' He saw it at the end of every little street and from the deserted Square rising up towards the sky, huge and indifferent. The streets were narrow and dirty like the alleys radiating from village churches. Here and there he noticed a red lantern over a doorway, the sign of an equivocal hospitality . . . Meaulnes felt his pain an anomaly in this unclean vicious quarter which, as in medieval days, took refuge under the very buttresses of the cathedral. He had a peasant's fear of, and a peasant's repugnance towards, this vast edifice where all the vices were carved in hidden corners, this church flanked by brothels and offering no remedy for the deep sorrows of a pure love . . .

Two girls going by, their arms round each other's waist, looked at him boldly. Half disgusted, half reckless, as if to take revenge on his love or destroy it, Meaulnes rode slowly behind them. One of the pair, a wretched girl with thin blonde hair drawn back into a false chignon, gave him a rendezvous for six o'clock in the Archbishop's garden – the garden where Frantz, in one of his letters, had made an appointment to meet poor Valentine.

He didn't decline, knowing that by six he would be miles away. And for some moments, from a low window in the steep narrow street, the girl kept waving her hand towards him.

He was anxious now to be off.

But before leaving the town he could not resist a gloomy desire to go by Valentine's house once more. He stared at it intently, as if to add this to his hoard of bitter memories. It was one of the last houses in the suburb, and the street trailed off into a country road. Opposite the house a vacant piece of ground formed something like a small Square. There were no faces at the windows, no one in the yard, nor in the street itself, except for an unkempt girl with a powdered face who walked past close to the wall dragging two ragged children behind her.

It was there that Valentine had spent her childhood, there where she had first looked out at the world with innocent, trusting eyes. Behind those windows she had worked and learned to sew. Frantz had come down this suburban street to see her, to smile at her. And now there was nothing left, nothing . . . The dreary afternoon dragged on, and Meaulnes imagined that somewhere, perhaps at this very moment,

Valentine was seeing in memory this sordid little haven to which she would never return.

The long journey ahead of him was to be the last respite to his sorrow, his last deliberate distraction before sinking into it for good.

As he rode away from the town, charming farmhouses appeared here and there on either side of the valley near the banks of the river, their pointed gables covered with green trellises showing through the trees. On their lawns no doubt girls were gravely exchanging love secrets. It was a setting for people with hearts and souls – innocent souls . . .

But for Meaulnes at that moment only one love existed, a love that had been met only half-way and then cruelly repulsed, and the girl whom of all others he should have protected and shielded from evil he had sent to perdition.

A few hasty lines of the diary indicated that he had resolved to find Valentine at whatever cost before it was too late. A date in a corner of the page seemed to indicate that it was for this journey Madame Meaulnes had been making preparations the day I turned up at La Ferté-d'Angillon and upset all his plans. In the deserted Town Hall on that fine morning of late August, Meaulnes had been jotting down his memories and projects when I pushed open the door and told him things he had given up all hope of hearing. He had been caught up once more in the old adventure, and paralysed, unable to act or to confess. And from that moment he was a prey to remorse, regret, and sorrow – at moments suppressed, at other moments dominant, until the day of his wedding when a theatrical cry from the woods recalled him to the first vow he had taken as a man.

In this same exercise-book he had hastily scribbled a few words at dawn, just before leaving – with her permission but for ever – the woman to whom he had been married only a few hours:

I'm going away. I must find the two vagrants who came to the fir wood yesterday and rode off towards the east on their bicycles.

I will not come back to Yvonne unless I can bring her brother and Valentine with me and see them married and lodged in Frantz's own house.

This manuscript, which I began as a secret diary and which has become a confession, will be the property of my friend François Seurel in case I should not come back.

He must have slipped the notebook under the others in his old school trunk, hastily turned the key in the lock, and disappeared.

EPILOGUE

TIME went by. I was giving up hope of seeing my companion again, and spent bleak days in the village school, or sad days in the deserted house. Frantz failed to keep the appointment we had agreed on. And my aunt Moinel knew nothing of Valentine's present address.

The one source of happiness Les Sablonnières had to offer was the little girl whose life had once hung by a thread. By the end of September it was evident that she would be a sturdy and a pretty child. She was now nearly a year old. Clutching the rung of a chair she would push it unaided, trying to walk, tumbling down and getting up again and making a din that reawakened old echoes through the lonely house. When I held her in my arms she would never let me kiss her. She had an untamed and yet a charming way of wriggling and pushing my face away with her open hand and screaming with laughter as she did so. Her gaiety and energy seemed destined to efface the atmosphere of grief that had clung to the house since the day she was born. I sometimes thought: 'For all her wildness, the day is bound to come when she'll be in a sense my own child.' But once again Providence decided otherwise.

One Sunday morning in late September I had got up very early, even before the peasant woman who took care of the baby. With Jasmin Delouche and two men from Saint-Benoist I was going off to fish in the Cher. I was on good terms with the villagers who often included me like this in their poaching expeditions – fishing with nets, which was prohibited, or, at night, by hand. In summer on my free days I would set off with them at dawn and not come home before noon. For most of these men this was their chief source of livelihood. For me, it was my one pastime, the only distraction that reminded me of former light-hearted excursions. And I had ended by acquiring a great liking for these long rambles, fishing along the river-bank or among the reeds of a great pond.

On that particular morning I was up at half past five and went out to a little lean-to by the wall separating the flower garden of Les Sablonnières from the kitchen garden of the farm. I was busy disentangling nets which I had thrown down in a heap the previous Thursday.

The sun was not yet up. In the twilight of the fine September dawn the shed in which I was hastily sorting my gear remained half in darkness.

I was rummaging about in silence when I heard the click of the gate and the sound of steps on the gravel.

'What a nuisance!' I thought. 'They're here ahead of time and I'm not ready.'

But the man coming into the garden was a stranger. He was, so far as I could make out, tall and bearded and dressed like any of the chaps I was expecting, but instead of coming to the lean-to where they knew I could be found at the time of our rendezvous, he went up to the front door of the house.

I thought: 'It's a mate of theirs they've invited without telling me, and they've sent him on as a scout...'

The stranger tried the handle of the door, quietly, cautiously. But I had locked it on coming out. So he tried the handle of the kitchen door. Then he hesitated for a moment, turned towards me, and I saw him full-face in the pale morning light. Only then did I recognize *le grand Meaulnes*.

For some time I stood still – frightened, despairing, helpless against the deep pain his return had suddenly reawakened. He had gone to the back of the house and now reappeared, still looking uncertain.

Then I went towards him, and embraced him, sobbing, unable to utter a word.

He understood at once:

'Then she is dead.'

He stood motionless, insensible, forbidding. I took him by

the arm and gently urged him towards the house. It was growing light. To get the worst over, I took him straight upstairs to the room in which she had died. He went over to the bed, fell on his knees, and for a long while remained with his head buried in his arms.

He got up at last, wild-eyed, stumbling, bewildered. And again taking his arm I led him into the next room which had become a nursery. The baby had woken up alone while the nurse was downstairs, and had propped herself up into a sitting posture in her cradle. All one could see of her was her head, as her eyes turned to look at us in surprise.

'Here's your little girl,' I said.

Then he picked up the child and held her in his arms. At first he could scarcely see her for tears. Then, as if embarrassed at his own tears and tenderness, though still holding the baby close to his breast, he turned to me and said:

'I've brought them both back . . . You can call on them in their own house.'

And in fact, later in the morning, as I walked thoughtfully, almost happily, towards the house which Yvonne de Galais had first shown me when it was an empty shell, I saw from a distance a young housewife in a white collar sweeping the doorstep, to the great wonderment and admiration of some young cowherds going off to Mass in their Sunday clothes . . .

Meanwhile the baby was getting bored at being held so tightly, and as Augustin, his head turned to hide or brush away his tears, failed to meet her eyes, she gave him a sharp little smack on his bearded mouth.

This time he lifted her high in the air, bounced her up and down, and looked at her with an attempt at laughter. That was enough, and she clapped her hands in approval . . .

I had stepped back to watch them. A little disgruntled and at the same time marvelling, I could see that the child had at last found the companion she had been unconsciously waiting for . . . I could see that *le grand Meaulnes* had come to take back the one joy he had left me. And already I pictured him, in the night, wrapping his daughter in a cloak, to carry her off with him on some new adventure.

MORE ABOUT PENGUINS

Penguinews, an attractively illustrated magazine which appears every month, contains details of all the new books issued by Penguins as they are published. Every four months it is supplemented by *Penguins in Print*, which is a complete list of all books published by Penguins which are still available. (There are well over three thousand of these.)

A specimen copy of *Penguinews* can be sent to you free on request, and you can become a regular subscriber at 30p for one year (with the complete lists) if you live in the United Kingdom, or 60p if you live elsewhere. Just write to Dept EP, Penguin Books Ltd, Harmondsworth, Middlesex, enclosing a cheque or postal order, and your name will be added to the mailing list.

Note: *Penguinews* and *Penguins in Print* are not available in the U.S.A. or Canada

ANDRÉ GIDE

STRAIT IS THE GATE
This description of young love blighted and turned to tragedy by the sense of religious dedication in the beloved is often regarded as the most perfect piece of writing Gide achieved.

THE IMMORALIST
The story of a man's rebellion against social and sexual conformity. The problems posed here are those which confronted Gide himself.

THE VATICAN CELLARS
Through this strange drama involving the alleged abduction of the Pope, a 'miraculous' conversion, swindling, adultery, bastardy and murder, Gide works out the idea of the unmotivated crime.

LA SYMPHONIE PASTORALE/ISABELLE
La Symphonie Pastorale explores the conflict between profane love and Christian charity. *Isabelle* evokes the atmosphere of a legendary romance, set in a Norman château.

FRUITS OF THE EARTH
This hymn to the pleasures of life reflects Gide's search for and discovery of bodily and spiritual joy.

JOURNALS 1889–1949
Here Gide recorded his sixty years of full and active life as teacher, naturalist, musician, moral philosopher, critic and novelist, and discussed the problems he faced in his major works.

Not for sale in the U.S.A.